DEFYING THE DRAGON PRINCE

ROYAL DRAGONS
BOOK TWO

SELINA COFFEY

LOVY BOOKS

Lovy Books Ltd
20-22 Wedlock Road
London N1 7GU
United Kingdom.

WILLOW

The sound of a crying infant pierced the quiet of the grove. I looked around at oak trees far more ancient than any I'd ever seen before. Their limbs were so old and thick that they rested on the ground. Green moss streamed from their top branches, and the breeze moaned through the forest.

I absorbed the scenery of the unfamiliar forest, amazed at the beauty of the place Malcolm's brother brought me to. Arista's child was crying in the distance, and I pitied the child that only wanted its mother. I studied the grove, feeling magic untamed as I turned away from the piercing cries. His father would be there to soothe him.

We'd all been terrified when Arista passed out after giving birth, but she'd soon awakened, refreshed and ready to name her child. Galen was the name they chose, because it meant peaceful and calm, just like their little son. He was a beautiful child, and now his mother and father were getting married in an old grove filled with ancient magic.

"Willow," that voice called out my name.

I turned to see Henry there, waiting for me. He irritated me with his charming smile and his arrogant manners.

He was my mate, but that didn't mean I had to like it. Oh, Arista thought I didn't know, but I did. He'd fascinated me the first time I saw him, but since then, as he hung around to heal me and keep his own strength up, I'd come to find he irritated me.

He always talked about how rich he was, how he could buy anything he wanted, and he'd been all over the world. I had nothing to compare that with. I could get him a gallon of milk and show him the Wal Mart twenty miles away, but that was it. I would often stare at him and wonder if he did it out of some odd habit, or if he thought the brags would attract me?

His charming grin was in place, flashing at me as he found me alone in the grove.

"It's all ready then?" he asked me, his gaze raking over me.

I felt the heat of desire but ignored it. I didn't want to feel desire for Henry, I just wanted to heal so I could get back to my real life and the real world. Arista might be on the way to her wedding, but that wasn't in my stars. I was meant for other things.

"Yes, as soon as the guests arrive." I spoke to him in a monotone voice, one that didn't invite further discussion, but also didn't tell him to piss off like I wanted to.

Not exactly, anyway.

"I'm going to have a wedding like this one day," he hinted, his eyes on me.

"That's only because of the..." I stopped myself before I went too far.

Maybe if we weren't mates I'd feel differently, but we were. I wanted love because it was driven by passion and need, not a physiological reaction to something fate decreed. Would he feel the same if he wasn't my mate? Would he still dream of weddings and the future?

I was healed now, I wanted to get back to playing the piano and composing symphonies. I didn't want to think about babies and weddings.

He came close, his eyes burned into mine.

"You can have your symphonies, Willow, and you can have your passion, if only you'd give in to what we can't deny." His words were a confrontation, a confrontation I didn't want to have right now.

I pushed him away, or rather, I tried to, but my hands only drew him closer. His eyes were so beautiful, and his lips, they looked so inviting.

I felt a shiver go down my spine as his hands ran

over my bare arms. Want filled me, and for the first time in my life, I didn't think I'd be able to say no to something. To Henry.

I moved closer to his lips, wondering how long it would be before the wedding guests arrived. Was there time to slip away, let him give me the physical satisfaction I craved, and then come back?

I waited, my lips parted in anticipation of this first kiss, and tried to make a decision.

"Willow? Arista needs you."

I turned away, the sound of Malcolm's voice a welcome interruption. He was dressed in a hunter green kilt with a white shirt and a hunter green jacket. He looked rather handsome, even if he was a dragon.

"Thanks, Malcolm. I'll go see what she needs. Bye, Henry." I didn't turn back, mainly because I was afraid if I did, I wouldn't leave.

I made my way to Arista inside of the cabin they'd set up for the wedding. She was in the bedroom, wedding gown on, hair done perfectly, and a veil of soft lace in place. She should be radiant but instead, she had tears in her light-brown eyes so like my own. We could be sisters we looked so similar. We were both tall with slim waists but full figures, and both had light-brown hair and light-brown eyes. She was a year older than me, and her nose tilted where mine was a straight shot all the way to the tip. I also had a rounder face than her.

"What's wrong, Arista?" I rushed to her side where she sat on the bed and took her hand. "Why are you crying?"

"I need to pee! I can't go on my own. Mom has Galen, your mom is with her, and Mary's outside some-where, I don't know where. Can you help me? It's so hard to do with this thing on! I can't hold all of the lace and silk and keep my balance!"

"Girl, come on. I'mma help you get your pee on." I put on a funny voice and it did the trick. Her tears dried up as she grinned.

"I'm sorry, I'm an emotional wreck today. It's only a wedding, I don't know why I'm like this." She dabbed at her eyes and I helped her clean around her eyes with a tissue. I touched up her makeup and stood her up.

"Come on, you have every right to be weird today, cuz. You're about to be a wife!" I gave her a hug, and then I helped her do what she needed to do before we made our way to the front porch. I could see, off to the right and in a glade, the place where we'd set up an arbor and seats for the guests. There weren't many, Malcolm and Arista both wanted a small wedding, after all. No more than two dozen people were invited.

A short while later, I watched my cousin walk up the aisle with a grin. Arista was my savior in the end, because she'd brought the dragon mate that I needed to survive to me. Even if I did hate him. I shot a glare over at Henry, who stood by his brother's side, and wondered how I was supposed to get through life shackled to him.

My mother, Rachel, hadn't needed a man to raise me, and she was actually happy with her life, man or not. For all I knew, Momma might have even liked women, but I doubt she needed a woman either. She was happy in her own little world, and that's how I was now that I was well again.

My fingers clenched as I thought about the piano in the house. It was an old upright piano, all we could afford when I'd first learned how to play, and it was always a comfort to run my fingers over the keys. Before I became ill with the mating-sickness—lack-of-being-near-my-mate-sickness—whatever it was called, I'd been on my way to a career in music.

Classical music, sometimes a gig in New Age came up, but I'd been on my way. I was a composer by training. I'd scrimped my way through a bachelor's degree for it, and now I was finally getting the flexibility back in my long-disused fingers. Maybe I could get back on track, maybe I couldn't, it remained to be seen. That led me back to Henry.

Another, less baleful glance, showed he had a huge grin on his face as the magical being that officiated the wedding droned on and on in a language I didn't understand. The man was a wizard of some sort with a long white beard that flowed down to around his knees over a purple robe with a face so wrinkled you almost couldn't see his eyes. In contrast, Henry had on a suit, black with a silver cummerbund, and he looked stunningly handsome.

I wished he wasn't my mate! If I knew he wanted me for more reasons than just this silly mate-bond that bound us together I might actually go for the guy. Well, no, I wouldn't, especially not when he started to brag about his material wealth. I'd grown up poor, but fed, loved, and nourished in all ways. Material wealth meant little to me. For that reason alone, I found most of what he said to be insufferable.

"And so, today, as I join these two magical beings into one, one with each other, and one with nature that gives us all we need, I ask you all to share in their joy," I heard the man say, but assumed he'd switched to English.

When none of the guests from my world reacted, I looked back at him.

"May you go into your future with peace and love, my children." I understood that too.

The people from my world looked confused as the guests from Malcolm's world applauded and stood up. What had just happened there? I'd either understood a foreign language or none of the guests had heard him. There weren't that many that they couldn't have heard his words spoken in a louder voice. Well, I'd just have to file that one away for later. For now, I had to follow along behind Arista as she and Malcolm left the dais.

They walked through the crowd but didn't stop for too long, only long enough to gather up baby Galen, accept a kiss or a handshake, and then they flew off together. They were headed straight for their honeymoon, apparently a dragon tradition, and the rest of us were left behind to mingle. The tradition was fine with Arista, she'd said, she wanted out of that dress as soon as possible anyway. I'd laughed at the time, but now I felt rather sad as I watched them fly away, Malcolm in his dragon form with Arista and Galen cradled just between his wings.

She was off to her new life now, and I'd only just got her back. Her father had taken her away when Arista was young, believing her mother was insane, and she'd come back to our town when she'd run out of answers for her own bad health. We'd both needed our dragon mates, though we hadn't known it then. That's why we had become so ill, ill to the point of death.

Now that Malcolm and Henry were around though, we were both healthier. The gray color had left my long hair, and my skin had gone back to its youthful elasticity. I'd looked 20 years older when Henry had first come around and seen the age illness had given me. Now, I was the 22-year-old we all knew me to be. If only I could maintain it without the dragon around.

I sighed deeply and went to find my mother. I saw Eve and Ted, Arista's parents, still in their chairs, their heads very close together. There was romance afoot there.

"That's been a long time in the making," my mother said quietly as she came up beside me.

"It has, Momma, it has. I still want to be mad at him for what he did, but I know it was all for Arista. He loved his daughter enough to try to protect her."

"It's a hard thing to forgive, but if Eve can do it, so can we." My mother took my hand and we went off to the area where food had been prepared by caterers from our world.

There weren't many people from my world, but there was some family who knew about the dragons, and a few people the magical world had brought along for the wedding. The rest were all from the magical world, but they'd been gracious in allowing us our own food. I mean, they're magical beings, they could force us to eat some magical cow or something, couldn't they?

I continued to ponder the food choices that could have been made as I walked up to a table and filled a plate with pasta salad and a yeast roll. I didn't want anything else just then, so I turned to leave the table and find a drink. I bumped into Henry but managed to save the plate.

"Careful now." He grinned as he held his hands out

steady me. His fingers gripped into my shoulders and, again, awareness flowed through me. "We don't want you to twist an ankle or anything."

"Thanks," I muttered and made to push past. I made it clear I didn't want to talk to him by storming away.

I cast a look back, just before I walked into the cabin, to see him still there, a confused look on his handsome face. Tall with black hair and green eyes, Henry was more than handsome, he was gorgeous. He knew it too. Arrogance, a fascination with material goods, boastful, but still somehow charming… he wasn't my type at all.

Not that I really had a type, but I knew he wasn't it. I let the screen door slam as I turned away from him and told myself to ignore the hurt on his face that soon replaced the confusion. It wasn't my fault we were mates. It also wasn't my fault he was such a dick. If he'd been a charmer, charitable, and helped old ladies across the street, I'd have loved him instantly. Instead, my prince was a giant toad.

Which reminded me that Arista was now a princess, and her own son a prince. Wow, I thought as I sat down. From hillbilly to princess just like that. The world that used to be so uncomplicated, so average and run of the mill, had become a place that left me confused, angry, and often bewildered. I didn't like it one bit, and unfortunately for Henry, I liked the idea of being a princess even less.

2

HENRY

She's a slippery little thing, my mate. I watched her head into the cabin and decided I needed a new tactic. My little honeybee hadn't melted over the nectar of my wealth as most human women did. Not that I'd come into contact with many, but I used to venture out into the human world in secret. Humans fascinated me. They should have easier lives than us magicals, but they always seemed to make everything *so damned complicated.*

It's not like they had wolf shifters out and about on the hunt for human females to kidnap and make babies with. Nope, that was just in my world, the shifter world that my father ruled. At least, in our kingdom. There were other shifter worlds, but this one was ours. We shifters were just the tip of the iceberg, and my brothers and I enforced the laws of that world. We *ruled* that world. My brother Malcolm was the head of our world's security force. As his second in command, I carried just as many burdens as he did, sometimes more because I had to carry out the wishes of my father, even above Malcolm's. That hadn't always made life easy—especially when Malcolm had defied our father and went to his human mate.

I brushed those thoughts aside and went to a table filled with drinks. At least father had insisted our own wine be brought to this ceremony. Our grapes were unique, with a distinct flavor that could only be found in the grapes of our world. There was something close to it in the human world, muscadine I believe it's called, but perhaps not. I poured a glass for myself, determined to leave my mate alone for a while as I decided on a new approach.

"Perhaps if you just stopped acting like an ass around her she wouldn't do her best to avoid you," my sister Mary's voice came from behind me and I turned to grimace at her.

"Hush, woman, I know what I'm doing." Mary might be a woman, but I knew she could kick my ass if I really pissed her off. She was a strong woman, but more importantly, she was a well-trained fighter, and she'd taken down men bigger than me despite her smaller stature.

"Bite your tongue, brother!" she said with a twist of

her own lips before she fluttered her eyelashes at me. "Or should I beg for forgiveness in the soft drawl of your human to calm you down?"

"My human indeed! You're right, I have no idea what I'm doing here. She hates me and only allows me around because of the mating-sickness." I had to admit the truth, even if it did hurt.

"Was it four castles you told her you owned, or just the one in Italy? I can't remember now."

"Have you been spying on me?" I scoffed, but my attempt to feign indignation failed as miserably as my attempts to woo Willow had floundered.

"It's my job to spy on our people," she said with a smirk. She was lucky she was my sister.

"Did father put you up to it?" He hated the humans, even if he did cave in to Malcolm's undeniable need for his bride.

"Maybe," she said and stirred the grass with the toe of her boot. She hadn't dressed for the wedding, she'd remained in her military-style black uniform with her combat boots. "Actually no, I was just nosy."

"You are so going to get it if you keep on!" I told her and wagged my finger to emphasize my point. "I don't know what, but you'll get it. Maybe a week of cleaning out the dungeons. Or the cesspit beneath the animal barns. Hmmm..."

Mary stared at me with disgust and horror and I

knew I'd won. "There, stop your spying and I'll let you off the hook. It's Malcolm's wedding day, I should be generous, I suppose."

"No wonder she hates you," Mary muttered.

We all loved each other dearly, my siblings and I, but we were also dragons, and we could be very hard on each other. To prove a point, or to teach a lesson, even if the lesson had started out as a joke. Mary would take whatever decision I made because that was our way. Technically, she had been in the wrong to spy on me. I would let it go, though. I had more important things on my mind.

"What am I doing wrong?" I needed her advice, not her spite now.

"Look at her, Henry. Does she look like a castle would impress her?" Mary's tone implied I might be deficient in the intelligence department.

"Well yes, it does actually, Mary. She's poor! What else will impress a poor woman?" I thought it was a logical conclusion to come to.

"Fucking hell," Mary spat out, her look of disgust back in place. "Really, Henry? Damn, you are a moron. I don't care if you put me in the cesspit for a month, you, Henry are a dumbass."

Oh, that's just wrong. A human insult?

"Excuse me?" My dragon snarled through my human voice as my anger flared.

"You heard me, dumbass. Total, undoubted moronic dumbass." She punctuated each word with a jab of her finger into the hard muscle of my chest. With her long nail, it kind of hurt. I backed away as she continued.

"Willow won't be impressed by riches or extravagance! She grew up where those things don't matter. She's never been to an Italian castle, and probably thought she'd never see one. She's not the kind of, of…" She stopped to find the right word. "Bimbo to be impressed by your wealth!"

"Then what will impress her, since you're an expert on humans and their terminology now?" I tamped down on my dragon and tried to see reason. Mary was being rude, but as she continued I saw she might just have a point.

"She'll be impressed if you ask her to play for you. And if you sit quietly and listen. I've heard her a few times when I came to arrange the wedding details. She's a master at it. It's unlike anything I've heard before."

"Play what exactly? Obviously you mean music, but what instrument?" I was a bit angry that I didn't know about this side of Willow. Why hadn't anyone told me?

"The piano, you dunce! You don't even know that much about her? And you want her to mate with you? Oh boy, you've lost your mind." Her eyes went wide as she turned away, their own message of "dumbass" loud and clear.

"Maybe I've approached this entirely wrong. She really plays the piano?" I had an idea in the back of my head, but it hadn't become a full idea yet.

"Yes, but I wouldn't call it playing. She makes it hers, she does incredible things with it. It's beautiful, really."

"Right. Let me think then. Are human pianos the same as ours?"

"Yes, why?"

"Just an idea. I'll see you later, sister. Enjoy your time in the cesspit." My parting shot was only a jest, but it got the reaction I expected. A bread roll whizzed by my head as I shifted and took flight.

My human brain stayed active as my dragon body flew through the sky. We magicals had cloaked ourselves from the humans long ago. It was a measure meant to protect us from them and them from us as both of our populations grew. Too many clashes happened, too many lives were lost, so we withdrew from that world. Now, we were being forced by some of our own to venture back into that world. Sure, we made the occasional foray into the human world for entertainment or to keep ties with those select few who knew about us, but generally we stayed in our world.

Dragon hunters, or slayers as they were sometimes called, were a mixture born of our early interactions and had been left behind in the human world. They were too dangerous to dragonkin, and so we'd eliminated them from our world. Now, fate was playing a huge joke on us all. Dragons had been mated to dragon hunters somehow, and that made life... interesting.

At least to me anyway.

I could see that Willow and Arista were similar in appearances, but their abilities as dragon hunters differed. Arista was calm around us. Willow always bristled, and I knew it was from far more than my presence. She couldn't relax around any dragon. Even when she appeared to let her guard down, I knew deep down she was still instinctively on alert.

The flight to my homeland didn't take long, just long enough to stretch my dragon muscles and to let my dragon brain take over for a little while. I tucked my wings in to dive down to the castle that had always belonged to my family and brought myself to a halt with a gentle flap of my giant black wings before I landed. A dragon with glittering, reptilian eyes took up the area the humans would call a launch pad. I could change my size to suit my own desires, and right now I was in giant form. A long tail flowed 30 feet behind me, covered in spikes along the length with two razor-sharp points at the end. This was my shape, I couldn't change that, but I could change my size.

With little more than a blink and a thought that flitted through my brain, I was a human again, or I appeared like a human anyway. Physiologically, I was a human in this shape. I just had the paranormal ability to turn into a dragon as well. This made my family and me the rulers of this land. Our inherited role as the rulers was one that could not and would not be changed. Father could choose any of his children to inherit his throne, but we all knew the firstborn child would be the one to take that role.

If Mary had been born first or had been the first of the children to survive to that point, she would inherit. As it was, that role would be filled by Malcolm, and the rest of us were there to impose the laws we all lived by. Laws chosen for us and enshrined on parchment a long time ago. Which led me to my next task for the day: find out more about these wolves who took it upon themselves to kidnap women. I strode through a door, down a long set of stairs, and down another until I reached the dungeons.

There a guard waited for me in a small limestone cell. A prisoner sat in a chair at a table, and a long chain around his wrists shackled him to the floor. The man was a wolf shifter, the latest caught as he attempted to kidnap a human female.

"Please tell me you didn't do this." I sighed as I turned the chair on the other side with the back to the table and straddled it. My suit was made well enough that it didn't impede my movement, but I probably should have changed into a uniform, just for the intimidation factor.

"You don't know what it's like for us, dragon." The young wolf, no more than twenty-one, growled from where his head rested on his folded arms. He brought his blond head up just enough to glare golden eyes at me.

"You're barely even out of your puppy stage and you're already desperate for a mate? From what I've heard about marriage, it's bad enough without your mate hating you because you took her ass from all she knows into a world that she's always been told is a nightmare."

"Yeah, well, it's my job to change that for my woman isn't it? Make her see that our way is the best way to live." He leaned back now, cocky and self-assured in his manhood.

I rolled my eyes, I didn't even try to hide it. "Look, Aleric, you're in a shitload of trouble, pretending to be some hard bastard won't get you anything but a longer sentence."

"It'd be the same out there without a woman to keep me company so what's the difference?"

"You can leave any time you want to, for starters? In here, you're stuck, and you won't get out. Believe me, you won't."

"Your brother did it, I can too, dragon." He made an

obnoxious noise by sucking his cheeks through his teeth, and I wanted to kick those same teeth in.

"Fine, stay. I don't really give a fuck. Let the guard know when you're ready to get out of here."

I had to follow my father's orders. I didn't like keeping other magicals in the dungeon for doing what we'd done so often in the past, but we couldn't take the risk on a human being brought here against their will, male or female. If they escaped and told the human world about us, there would be a battle on our hands. For now, I'd let the man barely more than a pup with whiskers rot in the dungeon until he saw sense.

I headed back to my own quarters, took a shower, and prepared to spend the night in quiet and peace. I needed to think about a better way to approach Willow. I'd failed miserably in my first attempts to bend her to my will. She didn't like the braggart who swaggered when he wasn't mooning over her. Would she want the bastard who ignored her and treated her like dirt, instead? I'd heard human women liked alpha asshole males.

Was that where I'd gone wrong?

A knock came at the door and I groaned as I answered it. "What now?"

A woman stood there, a human woman in tears, held in place by a guard with a grip on her elbow.

"We found this human in a wolf lair, sir. What do we

do with her?" He spoke in our language, but she understood him.

"I just want to go home! I won't tell anyone, I swear. I'm pregnant, and I just want to go home to my family and to have my baby in a nice clean hospital. Mac promised I could go home any time I wanted to! Why am I being held prisoner?"

I watched her as she spoke, astonished. She didn't even realize she'd spoken our language, a language almost impossible for humans to learn. Unless they were female and pregnant with a shifter child.

"I'm sorry, your unborn child is a shifter. The baby belongs here, not in your world. You'll both have to stay here." I paused, angry that I had to say the next words. I did my duty, though and turned back to the guard. "Put her in the dungeon, but give her a nice cell with a bed, will you? She is pregnant with a shifter, after all."

She still hadn't realized I hadn't spoken in English, nor had she for that matter, and I felt terrible for her. She just wanted to go home, but she could never go back again. Her male wolf might have told her she could, to bring her here willingly, but he'd lied to her. He'd have to deal with that shit, it was only my job to deal with the fact that she and her child existed at all. That was more than enough.

3

WILLOW

I could feel the weakness that always came when it had been too long since I'd last seen Henry. We usually met twice a week, on Sunday evenings and on Thursday evenings. I hadn't seen him since Arista's wedding the week before. I could only assume he'd been busy, too busy for his own health. I had no idea what he did in the dragon world. Arista had only ever been interested in explanations about Malcolm, and the others in his group weren't talkers either.

Maybe he was off on some princely foreign trip. Foreign relations. Were there foreigners in his world? Was his land that big? I wondered, but then decided that he probably didn't do a lot; all of the bragging he'd done hinted at a man who loved to spend his wealth, not earn it. I played a note on the piano, an expression of my own inner turmoil, not really an attempt to create a new melody. Mom was at Eve's, my cousin Arista's mother's house and wouldn't be irritated by the noise.

I giggled as the note set something free inside of me, some long-held frustration, and I bashed at the keys ungracefully without any kind of rhythm. I felt as if each stabbing thrust of my fingers banged out a little more of my frustration, and I picked up the tempo, until I was wild, and screamed out just how frustrated I was! God, how I hated this all!

I couldn't stand the man, yet, my body had to be near him. When he was near, I craved more, I wanted so much more. Even my brain would sometimes start to overlook just how much I couldn't stand him and remind me how handsome he was. I just wanted it all to end because I was a wreck emotionally. I might be much better physically, but emotionally, this had all taken a toll that could be far more damaging than going without him had been.

By the time my frustration was spent and my throat was raw from the drawn-out screech, I was exhausted and leaned my arms against the top of the keys to rest my head. How could I make this all end? It wasn't fair, it wasn't fair at all! I wanted my life back, the one that had a defined path, with goals that I'd only just started to meet. Not this travesty that saw me in a hate-to-love relationship with a magical, mythical being. What the hell, fate?

I felt a change in the air, a subtle breeze that wasn't real but still tangible, as my body responded to Henry's nearness. He was somewhere nearby then, I just didn't know where. I'd come to recognize the sensation shortly after he first appeared in my life. My body healed every second he was near me and it deteriorated every second he was away. When we came close enough to each other the damage would start to reverse, and I could feel it within my body as a slight breeze blew away the ashes of the damage.

Speak of the devil…

How close was he? Had he heard the concerto of pain I'd just played? Would he know it was me that had trilled through the keys as I released the anxiety and rage my new life caused me? Or would he assume it was something I listened to? We hadn't really talked about our lives or what we did with them. We'd barely spoken to each other at all.

I went outside to try to find him before he came into the house and unnerved me even more, and found him in his dragon form up in a tree outside of the piano room. I looked up at him, no more than two feet tall, and squinted.

"You're not very scary looking." The words came out before I could stop them.

He changed instantly into a huge dragon that took up around 60 feet of space at the bottom and much more in height. I looked up, and up, and then up some more. In a move that made my head spin, he shifted into his human form.

"Not as frightening as that music you were playing just now, but I suppose I have my moments." Green eyes twinkled in the sunlight, his black hair just long enough to fall into his eyes as he tilted his head to the left. "Will you play something else for me?"

"Fuck off" came to mind immediately, but I bit my tongue. With a loud breath to calm my nerves, I looked at him speculatively. "I doubt I know anything from your land."

"Probably not, I don't think human hands can play our instruments." He sat down cross-legged against the tree and looked up at me with a cheeky grin, one that said he was about to rile me up and loved every moment of it. "Your instruments *are* inferior, but you make the best with what you have, I suppose."

I turned and walked away. I wasn't about to give him the satisfaction of taking his bait. I wanted to tell him to go home and listen to his superior music but didn't. I needed him to stay for at least a few more minutes to finish the process that healed us both. Then he could fly off back to his own world.

"Willow?" He was right behind me and I had been so caught up in my thoughts that I hadn't noticed.

"What?" I growled the words at him without a glance back.

"Will you play something else for me?" He repeated his earlier question, and I stopped. My left eyebrow quirked as I turned to look at him again.

"Why?"

He chewed at his lip for a minute and squinted in the direction of the sun. Was it that hard to come up with a reason?

"I liked what you played earlier, but it was angry, full of rage. I'd like to hear you play something calmer. You're very good, you know?" That strong jaw of his was well-defined as he leaned his head to the right, just enough for me to punch him.

Instead, I took another deep breath and walked back into the house. He followed me into the room, bare except for the piano, my stool, and a plain pine rocking chair Mom had put into the room to sit on when she'd come to listen to me play. Henry settled his long frame into the rocker without another word.

I went to the piano and began to play a piece by Beethoven, one that always calmed me but also moved me, a conundrum of its own. I couldn't watch Henry as I played, not without a turn of my head, so I didn't look. I had no idea what to expect when the last note filled the room. I turned around, too curious not to, and my mouth fell open.

He looked... astounded.

That was the only word for it. I waited, unsure why it mattered but for some reason, I needed to know that Henry liked how I played.

"What was that?" He looked directly at me, his eyes intense and filled with something I couldn't define.

"That was Beethoven. He was a composer during the late 18th century and early 19th century. He started to lose his hearing when he was in his 30s and was deaf by the time he died." I had to pause as Henry made a noise of disbelief. "I know, hard to believe isn't it? In fact, the piece I just played, the Moonlight Sonata, was composed with notes in the low tones, which were the only sounds he could hear by that point."

"Are you quite sure?" Henry didn't look like he believed me.

"Oh yes, he was quite deaf by the end. Oddly enough, Moonlight Sonata seems to be his most well-known piece of work in the world today. At least by the younger generations in America." I smiled, knowing there was more than one movie to blame for that.

"It was a beautiful piece of music. I can understand why it is still so loved, even after all of this time." He paused as if to think before he spoke again. "It's very... moving."

"It is." The notes replayed in my mind, the dour sounds haunted me, grief and doom mixed into a sound that was still somehow calming. How do you describe that?

I looked at Henry and realized why I'd played the piece. He reminded me of that song, the way he made me feel reminded me of the same emotions that piece of music stirred inside of me. It was like I was two different people, schizophrenic or my own doppelganger. All I know is at the same time he made me feel like I was in love, he also filled me with hate and irritation. It was about to break me.

"You know you don't really hate me, don't you? That's your dragon slayer twisting your mind." Henry spoke as if he could read my thoughts.

I cut my eyes to him, and for the first time, I really saw the man, not the enemy dragon, not my mate, but a person. He'd called me out with his words and made it all real. He'd brought my own inner turmoil out into the open and I felt as if he'd laid my soul bare with this new approach.

"I don't know what it is, but I do know I feel like I'm going crazy." It was the first real thing I'd admitted to him. I couldn't look at him, it was too much, too overwhelming to let him see me. In that moment, everything changed for me.

I heard him gasp and looked back up at him. What had he seen, what had I given away? I saw wonder on his face. "You are beautiful, Willow."

"Physical beauty fades," I warned him, but the words also served to fend off the compliment.

"I didn't mean your appearance. I meant who you are, Willow. The woman who made a box of wood and strings sing beautiful songs, the woman who cares about her family, the one who wants to take care of all of them, but never complains, even when it's too much." He was perched on the edge of the rocker, and his sturdy black leather boots drew my attention.

Why were those things so sexy? My eyes were drawn up the rest of him, covered in his black uniform, the cargo pants tight on his thighs and in other, more deli-cate places. That was just cruel, I thought to myself, while my eyes continued to move upwards. Crushing such sensitive parts in tight cotton should be against the law. My eyes didn't stop their travels and went up over a taut stomach that I knew would be as hard as a rock, over chest muscles filling the uniform out with round strength, and up to his shoulders.

He didn't move throughout my visual examination, he just stayed still and let me have my fill of him. I studied the length of his neck, long enough to fit my face into for kisses, for me to inhale the scent of him. I breathed deeply through my nose and wasn't surprised to find my head filled with his smell. I knew his scent by now.

I felt something stir in my chest as I found his dark red lips, full and dry. They needed kisses to moisten them and make them smooth. My fingers itched to touch them, to feel their softness. I had to suck in a deep breath into my own now dry mouth before I could move away from those lips. They drew me to him, and I didn't quite realize it, but I was up and in front of him before I knew it. My fingers traced down the hard line of his jaw while my eyes looked up to those green eyes.

Sometimes the color of grass, sometimes a more golden color, his eyes changed with his emotions. They were a dark green now, the color of the forest at twilight, and I knew he felt the same as me. Like there was no use in a fight I wouldn't win anyway. My fingers ran down the smooth line of his jaw and I felt my heart as it raced in my chest. I wanted... him. I wanted all of him, I wanted him to consume me in kisses that stole my ability to breathe, I wanted him pressed so far into me there was no us, only one. His fingers came up to slide down my cheek and the moment broke for me.

I sucked in the air I'd forgotten to breathe and pulled away. I needed to escape, I needed room to breathe, I need to *run.*

"You don't need to run, Willow. Come with me." He took my hand and pulled me back out of the front door and to the yard. "Just climb between my shoulders and hang on. I'll make you feel better."

I couldn't say no, there was some *need* within me that I could not understand, I couldn't even give it a name other than need. It crushed my chest, it gnawed at my brain, and I just needed. Fuck, it almost hurt I needed it so much! Henry shifted then, a blink and a swish of air, and then he was a dragon. Small enough to climb up on at first, he swiftly grew, and my perch between his shoulders became almost a cocoon. He climbed into the sky with a flap of leathery wings and soon we were high above the trees.

The wind blew through my long hair, pushing it from my face and around my neck if I sat up. The wind streaking over me seemed to soothe the hate within me, so I sat up and let it tear it all out of me. I started to laugh as he flew us through the sky, a laugh that turned into a scream at one point, but the wind screamed louder. I let it all out into the sky as we flew. I screamed and laughed until there was nothing left inside of me to scream or laugh about and fell onto his back, exhausted.

I gripped onto thick skin covered in plates of scales so wide one was enough for my bottom. Henry's wings tore through the air, and he kept going, he flew until I finally relaxed, and my body finally felt at peace. I didn't even know I'd fallen asleep cradled between his shoulders until he landed gently, and a shiver passed through his body. I sat up, saw that it was dark, and wondered what would happen next. I felt as if anything was possible now.

4

HENRY

I might have made a mistake. Maybe.

I'd felt Willow's disquiet as a buzz in the pit of my stomach. It had grown within my abdomen until it felt like a storm raged there. The idea to fly her into a soothed state had been a split-second decision, one made in the panic of the moment. Now, with her in my arms, her body soft against mine, I knew she was much calmer, but she still wasn't entirely certain about me.

I let her down when she stirred, her brain now on full alert. We shared a mental bond, but she didn't realize that yet. She'd blocked my communications and didn't even know. She was strong, very strong, but the fact that she was a dragon hunter mated to a dragon was about to break her. Perhaps I should have stayed outside and not insisted she play for me. Maybe she wasn't ready for this yet. Then she looked up at me, her eyes sparkled in the moonlight, and I forgot about mistakes.

Nothing about anything I did with Willow could be wrong, ever. She looked vulnerable in the cold light of the moon, as if her whole world depended on whatever I chose to do next. As a man, there was only one thing I could do when a woman like Willow looked at me like that.

I pulled her tight to my chest and found her lips with mine. Desire flared through me, and a groan of need vibrated from my throat. She tasted so fucking good! Damn, how could one woman taste like everything I'd ever wanted? Her lips were soft, pliant, and when my tongue flicked out they parted for me. I was hard by then, but I grew even harder when my tongue found the hot depths of her mouth. I'd never felt so much pleasure from a kiss, I've never felt so much need explode into life.

I picked her up and carried her onto the porch of the one-story home and found exactly what I needed when I reached the door. Our lips never broke apart as I pressed her into the hard wood, but it grew deeper when her legs wrapped around my waist and her hands tangled in my hair. I felt her fingers tense on the black strands as a bolt of pleasure, not pain at all.

Her fingers pulled at my head, and I let my head fall back. We were both out of breath, and I saw the way her light brown eyes turned just a shade darker. I panted until I'd caught enough breath to form words. "You know your playing soothes my dragon? The way I soothed your soul with flight, that's what your playing does for me."

"And my kisses, what do they do for you, dragon?" This was a different Willow. One that was in control, coquettish, and flirty. I liked her, a lot!

"Your kisses are a drug I may not be able to live without. Can I get a lifetime prescription for them?"

"We'll see." Her legs tensed around my waist and she pressed her core into my hard length. We both hissed as the pressure increased the ache inside of us but all I could see was that smile. Willow's brain had begun to open to me, and I think she heard my inner thoughts.

"You want me on my knees, do you?" She gave me a smirk, not surprised at all at the picture that had formed in my head when she'd pressed into me with that rather dirty smile.

"I want you every way I can have you, Willow. On your knees, on your back, over me, under me, however you want it. So long as I get to have you." I wasn't used to giving in but with Willow, I had to take what I could get, and I knew it. There was no single alpha here, there was only us.

"I don't want to think about it, Henry. Just..." Her words trailed off, and her eyes fixated on mine again as her index finger traced down my jaw to the square point of my chin. "Just make me not think. Make me feel."

"I can do that, princess." The endearment slipped out, and it seemed right. She was my princess, whether we'd mated yet or not. She would always be the only woman for me, from now on.

The moment seemed to slow down as I held her there, pinned against the door by my hips. She was perfect, beautiful, and so alluring with those eyes. There was innocence in them, but I also saw want, and a knowledge of exactly what it was she wanted. Was she a virgin? We'd never discussed anything of a personal nature, she'd never allowed it. I searched her mind and found only me there, only thoughts about what she wanted to do and with me.

One image in particular made me gasp and push my lips back to hers. The image of my head between her thighs, as she leaned against the door, one leg over my shoulder as she... but I had to put that image away for now or I'd lose it before I even had my hands against her skin. The thought of hearing the sounds she made as my tongue slicked over her opening was just too hot to let it go on.

It was definitely something I wanted to do at some point.

"You know what's going to happen if you let me inside the house, don't you, Willow?" I had to know, I had to have her consent. I didn't want her to give in just because she couldn't stand it anymore, I wanted her to want *me*.

"Yes, Henry. I know. You're going to fuck me."

"I'm not just going to fuck you, Willow, I'm going to make every inch of you mine. And give you every inch of me." Our eyes burned into each other, and I saw the sparkle of gold in her eyes. Her dragon hunter might be subdued for now, but it was still there, with all of the magic that brought to her. She didn't know what kind of magic yet, but she would, eventually.

I ran a finger down her cheek and felt the softness of a healthy woman there. When I'd first seen her, she'd been nearer to death than life. Her body had been frail and thin because the rich food her mother fed her wasn't the nourishment she'd needed. Only I could give her that. Now her frame was filling out once more and the weight added a softness to her that hadn't been there before.

"I want you to be really sure, Willow. I don't want you to go into this because your body tells you that you have to."

I knew I'd pushed my luck with that. I'd felt how intensely she'd hated me when I first arrived, but that had changed the moment I dropped the snobbish facade. I gave her the real me and hopefully, she'd give me what we both needed in return. We both healed when we were close to each other, it kept us alive and we survived, but not being properly mated to her, in every sense of the word, was killing me in its own way. It was killing her too, she was just too torn to notice.

"I... I don't know, Henry." She looked away then, and I let her body slide away from mine. Her uncertainty was enough to make me step back. She had to be sure, I meant it.

"Why not?" I wanted to talk her through it all, not nag her, and my question was more a lead than anything.

"I'm just... confused." She leaned back against the door and thumped her fist against it. "One minute I'm human but ill, and oh I have this crazy aunt who believes in dragons. Then my cousin comes back with the same sickness as me, and then these dragons show up, and it's all just so insane!"

"I can see how that would be frustrating." I wanted to take her hand to reassure her, but I didn't want to push her again.

"I don't think you can. You don't have this innate hatred of the man you want more than anything you've ever wanted before tearing you apart like I do. You can't know how that feels." She looked down at her own feet and put her hand over her mouth. I don't know if it was to stop the flow of words or something else. I thought I saw the sparkle of tears in her eyes before she stopped.

"Do you want to just stay out here, Willow? Will that make it better?" I'd be just as happy to be between her thighs on the ground than in a bed, but I wouldn't admit it. I'd just try to keep myself calm. The heartbreak in her voice, the raw pain, would stop me from trying to take advantage of the situation. She was right, I couldn't understand where she came from, but I could respect it. I expect, more than anything, the one gift I could give Willow that she'd appreciate the most was my respect for her.

"No. I don't want that. I want you to come in my house, and I want you to..." She stopped, and her bravado slipped a little. She'd tilted her face back up to mine and had stared into my eyes. Her lips moved but she didn't say words. "I need you, Henry. I can't deny that. Not having you is more painful than the hate I feel. I just can't decide which one is right. I do know the pain of not having you hurts a lot more than my hate does, though. Please, come inside with me."

I couldn't turn those brown eyes down, now could I? If she wanted me, I'd give me to her. Simple as that. I gave her a shy smile that quickly turned cheeky. "If that's what you want, Willow."

I wasn't a weak man, nor was I the swaggering brag-gart I'd shown her early on. I'd thought that was what she'd want, being a human and all. Now, I knew differently, and Mary's words came back to me. What did

Willow want? She didn't live in an expensive house, I took that to mean she'd want more. Now, I looked at it all with new eyes as she led me into the living room.

It was comfortable, warm, and inviting. It wasn't ostentatious and cold, a scream of wealth and a demand for respect. Willow and her mother valued family and people, not money or things. From the plaques on the wall that spoke of how love of family came above all, to the crocheted afghans spread over every chair and both couches in the living room, the room was a testament to all that these women valued.

I thought about the small room in the back of the house clad in pine, the room with hardwood floors and Willow's piano. It was empty except for the few pieces of furniture. It was a room meant for practice, a room without distraction or unnecessary items to dull the roll of the music she played. She composed her own too, I knew from Mary.

"Will you play for me again, Willow?" I asked, just in case she wanted to take a moment to compose herself. I liked the music she played, hearing more of it wouldn't be a bad thing.

"If you'd like. I'd rather take you to my bedroom." Her eyes were steady now. They didn't shy away or leave me to wonder about what she meant.

"Then lead on." I held my hand out in broad sweep and smiled at her with warmth.

My desire was tamped, for now, but only a glance or single word could bring it back to life.

To my surprise, she took my hand and pulled me down a short hallway to a dark part of the house. There were three closed doors, one to her mother's room on the left, a bathroom at the back, and her room on the right. It was all a bit rustic in Willow's home; unvarnished wood slats fitted together to form the thin walls, but the floor had been sanded and polished over time to shine. Willow's door opened, and I almost expected a room of whites and pinks, filled with light.

Instead, her room was dark, made even darker by blackout curtains and darkly varnished oak. The antique dresser, wardrobe, and her bed were all handmade from the same oak tree from the looks of it, as were the end-tables on both sides of her bed. Two black throw rugs protected sensitive feet from the cold floor. I went to the other side of the antique but beautiful bed and looked across a dark brown and hunter green handmade quilt at her.

"Are you quite sure, Willow? I don't want to rush you." I wanted to give her one last opportunity to say no. I doubted either of us would be able to say no once we'd started.

She looked at me, and before I could even gasp, she was over the high mattress and knelt in front of me, her face tilted up to me.

"I've never been more sure of anything, Henry. Take this need from me. Make this violent itch that won't be satisfied go away. Please."

Who was I to turn down such a beautiful plea for mercy? I ran my finger over her lips and stared down at her for a moment to savor that expression. I wanted it etched into my memory forever, the way she knelt there in front of me, her lips slightly parted, her eyes on fire for me and only me. I wanted to make sure I'd never forget how beautiful she was when she begged me to make her feel better. Just in case she did change her mind.

5

WILLOW

J crawled to him, for in that moment I was broken. I couldn't deny the part of me that longed for him anymore. His face was a work of art, his body beneath his black uniform a sculpture that many would envy, and his scent was the most wonderful thing I'd ever smelled. I needed to touch him, to feel him, to be a part of him. Nothing else would do.

I didn't want to be subjugated by him, I wanted to be him. I wanted him to be me. He watched, his finger on my lips, as I pulled the shirt from the waist of his pants. I wanted to tear the buttons from the shirt with a violent rip, but I undid each one slowly. My fingers trembled as I reached the last one and opened the panels. I rose on my knees, our faces only centimeters apart, and pushed the fabric from his shoulders. I felt the silk of his skin through my sensitive fingertips and closed my eyes. His skin was so *soft.*

I'd never been intimate with a man before, I'd always been too focused on learning, playing, and then I'd become ill. It wasn't a religious choice or a choice based on morals, I'd just never taken the time to feel desire for anyone before. Now, it wasn't a choice to feel desire, but it was a choice to act on it. I felt a smile dance along my lips when I glanced up at his eyes before I slid my hands over the hills of hard muscles of his chest, down his rib cage, along his narrow waist, over a flat, but hard abdomen. The muscles there popped and made ridges for my fingers to climb.

Every inch of him was perfect, even the area on his right side where a long, thin scar interrupted the smoothness. I looked at him with a quirked brow, and he smiled.

"A fight with a wolf a long time ago. It was much longer, but it healed well." I wondered just how old he was but decided to ask later. Right now, I wanted to explore Henry's body. Later, I would ask questions. The need to feel more of him against me—his naked skin against mine—overwhelmed me, and I swiftly pulled my own top from my body.

A twist and a flick of my index finger released my bra and I threw it behind me. Henry watched me, his breath steady until I removed the black lace. Then he began to breathe much quicker, and his eyes dropped. I pulled up his hands and placed them over the globes that more than filled his hands.

"Touch me, Henry. Make this pain go away." It was a plea, but also a directive. This is what I wanted. No more indecision, no more fighting with myself. My dragon hunter self could fuck right off, I wanted Henry far more.

The real Henry, the one who'd offered comfort and release, not the bragging little douche he'd originally presented himself as. The man who gave me solace, who asked me to play music for him, who told me it soothed his inner animal. I needed this god of perfection before me.

My eyes closed when his palms engulfed my breasts, but they flew open again when his fingers trapped my dark red nipples. Pleasure coursed from the tips all the way down to my... there. I felt my cheeks flame, and he smiled a smile so dirty my *down there* twinged again.

"Does that make your pussy pulse, Willow?" Oh, he didn't know who Beethoven was, but he knew our naughty words for our private parts? That made my lips quirk. "Of course I know those words, Willow, who do you think invented them?" His smirk was raw sexiness, but his words made me tense.

I narrowed my eyes at him, can you read my mind? I

thought the words, but he smiled before he looked into my eyes.

Of course I can read your thoughts, Willow. You're my mate.

How wide can your eyes go? Mine tested the limits as I heard his voice *in* my head for the first time. *How long?* I asked. He didn't even have the grace to look guilty when he answered.

Since we met. You'd have heard me long before now, but you were too frightened to allow it.

I squinted again. *I'm not afraid, I hated who you showed me in the beginning. There was no way I'd have ever been attracted to that man.*

He looked disgruntled at that but gave a twitch of his eyes as he thought at me once more. *I suppose you were right to hate him. That isn't me. At all.*

Then who are you, Henry? Show me?

There was no way for me to turn back now, this was going to happen. Good thing I didn't want anything else. I tilted my head and waited, my eyes wide as he looked me over. Would this be as good as my body promised it would be? Would this hold up to the promise of those romance novels I'd read on the sly? Would he rock my world and make me beg for more?

"All of that, and more, Willow." He didn't need to speak but did anyway.

I didn't want to wait anymore, so I didn't waste time

with a response. I pulled his face to mine and bent backward to bring him over me. I hissed in a breath when his hot skin crushed against my nipples, and sighed when his hips cradled between my thighs. That's what I needed. Pressure there, on that spot every book I'd read called my clit. The place only I'd ever touched before.

His lips dragged against mine, sucked at them as his hand pulled my right leg up to move my center tightly to his. I rocked my hips and gasped his name when a bolt of wonder shocked through me.

"You're going to make yourself come before I even get your pants off, Willow. Greedy girl." He spoke the words against the corner of my mouth before he nipped at my lip playfully. Then he thrust his cotton-covered cock into my pulsing core and I forgot how to breathe.

"More..." I gasped the word against his cheek as he glanced down to where our bodies pressed together. "I want more, Henry."

"And you'll get it, Willow, in good time. If you want your world to turn upside down, you'll have to wait for it. Flames burn hotter when you build a promising base, right?" His fingers traced down my jaw, over my collarbone, and down to a nipple that twisted into a tight bud when his fingers closed over it.

"Henry..." His name was a breath, it was pleasure spoken, and I gave myself up to him completely. I didn't care what he did, how long it took, I just wanted him to make me feel. I'd spent so long locked inside of my own dying body, and now I felt alive again. I wanted to feel life, to experience it. I didn't want to just witness the world around me, I wanted to be a part of it.

His hands traveled down to the curve of my waist and his head followed. That's when his lips closed over a tip burnished dark red from my desire. His hands steadied my hips, easing their bucking as I lost the ability to control my own body. He guided them into a rhythm that wasn't familiar, or even artful, but it was seductive. It felt seductive, and right, as we pressed together, over and over, close then apart. His lips tugged at the nipple in his mouth, hard, on the edge of pain, before he left it to find the other.

His hands grasped at me, guided me, as he thrust into my center still covered by my pants. I followed his guidance and my body began to feel like liquid swelling in a lava lamp. In places it bulged, in others, it thinned out to a breaking point. I began to pant—something was about to happen, something was about to break.

"Willow." He gasped my name against my nipple before he sucked at it, hard, and broke through the edge that fell into pain. It was so good, though, it made me *feel* and it was so good. Something broke apart within me as he bit at the bud, something that didn't give a fuck, and exploded in a pulse of black that blinded me to everything. The world ripped apart and became the two places he touched, my nipple and my center.

It wasn't just my clit, my walls gulped for him as pleasure rocked me, and I knew that I'd come even harder once he was inside of me. For now, it didn't matter, and a growl escaped me as he continued to torment me. Another wave broke over me, and I gasped again. My hands clenched in the quilt my mother had made for me, and my feet dug into the bed to match the thrust of his hips against mine.

I wanted music, I wanted something that matched what I felt, and sighed when I heard a sound unlike anything I'd ever heard before. Henry thought of a song from his own land, a sound that made my body respond as equally as his touch did. That's what finished me off at last and I was gone, into the void again, only this time that void was white, a negative reversed.

And I still had my pants on!

The world came back into focus eventually, and I looked down my own body. We were still clothed! I gave him a grin that was tired yet filled with wonder. "That was just so..."

"Extra?" he asked, with that cocky grin in place once more.

I laughed, I couldn't help it. "Where did you hear that?"

"I saw it on something called a social network. It

seems right for the moment."

"Yeah, it is." I laughed quietly, more out of shock. Yeah, he'd rocked my world.

"Shall we turn it upside down now?"

"Yes, please." I could see him through the dark curtain of my eyelashes and smiled. Mom was out for the night, we had hours of alone time together. I wanted to find out how much more "extra" he could make me feel.

"Get those pants off." He growled the word against my stomach as he moved down, then stood up. He kicked off his boots, and then slid his pants away.

"Whoa." That was going to hurt.

"What?" He looked down to the spot where my eyes were glued. "It's just my dick."

"Yeah, but, whoa. Are all men built like that in your world?" I eyed him, not sure how he was still conscious. If all of his blood was in that huge dick, then he must be light-headed.

"I'm actually on the average side in my world. Are your men so small that this is huge for you?" He looked down uncertainly, his left eyebrow crooked.

"You are *not* small. Not in any way. Fuck." I reached out for him and he moved onto the bed. He came up beside me, and I took him in my hand.

I'll never be able to take all of this, I thought, and heard him laugh. "We'll take it slow, princess. You'll take it all. You're a slayer, you can take anything my world can give you."

"I hope you're right." I wasn't so sure, especially when my fingers wouldn't meet around the space just beneath the tip of him. I let my hand glide down the length and smiled when he hissed in a breath. "Like that?"

"It's not an expert touch, but the fact that it's you makes it so much better." The truth at least.

I pulled my hand from him and touched the tip with my index finger. Hard but spongy. Would it feel the same in my mouth?

"No, don't, you can't do that to me right now, Willow. Maybe later. Maybe after I've fucked you into oblivion a few dozen times, but right now, you can't wrap those beautiful lips of yours around me or I'll come undone in your mouth."

"What would be so bad about that?" I shot back, my lips moving to him, I just wanted a taste, to feel him. Just once.

"Nothing, but it's not where I want to come. I want to be here, deep inside of you." His fingers went between my legs, straight into my wet depths. He drove into my tight walls without resistance. I was too slick for that.

I let go of his dick and fell back on the bed. His fingers fucked into me, fast and hard. They hit *that* spot, the one I'd doubted existed, before he slid another one into me. Three fingers opened the petals of my flower to him, and my legs fell open. I didn't want his fingers, I wanted him.

"Are you sure? We can do this in other ways."

"I want you to fuck me, Henry. Now." I was past the point of wanting to be teased. I wanted him inside of me.

He pulled me around to face him and slid his hands under my ass. With a sigh, he pressed his dick to my opening, and began a slow sink into my depths. I gasped as he stretched my untried walls. A deep breath forced him a fraction deeper, and his hands gripped my ass tightly as he reacted.

"I might die." He breathed the words out, and I glanced down to see I hadn't even taken the head yet. Eleven more inches to go, at least.

I felt full, as if I was already filled with him, but I wasn't. I dug my feet into the bed behind him and pushed myself onto him a little more. Another spark of pain, and a groan of pleasure from him.

"Fuck yeah, I'm so going to die. Hurry, Willow. Take it all before I die."

I knew I could torture him and take it slow, but I wanted to know too much.

I pushed hard, fast, and sank down onto all of him. *Now* I was full, now, oh God, now I was going to die with him. So much Henry, all of Henry.

6

HENRY

She was an angel. She had to be, how else could that tight sheath take my entire length? She closed around me, tight, slick, and hot: absolute perfection. I never wanted to leave her body, not even for the sweet temptation of her mouth. I only wanted to fuck this pussy, every second of my life, until I died. I didn't even care if I died in the process, this was all I'd ever wanted.

I've fucked women before, my own and human women, but this—fuck!—she was so tight around me. It made my balls ache and my stomach tense. I didn't want to move, I was afraid I'd come the moment I did. I gritted my teeth because Willow decided to *move*.

"Fuck, stop," I ground the word out between clamped teeth. "No, don't stop."

I couldn't make my mind up. Having her move

herself on my dick was torture, but when she stopped suddenly it was even more torturous. I flexed my hands on her ass, gripped the tight muscles, and gave her a pace to follow. I couldn't move, or I'd take over and I might forget myself. My dragon wanted to fuck, it wanted to split her open and fuck her until it found oblivion, but slayer or no, she was a woman, and deserved to get off too.

I flipped us on the bed, let her take the lead. I had to smile when a look spread over her face that lit my imagination. She was in control and knew it. Long hair brushed at my thighs as she tilted her head back and moved her body. I wanted to wrap my fists in that silky mass of hair, but instead I pulled my legs up to give her something to lean against, and then took her full breasts in my hands. I kneaded the soft flesh and she smiled. When I pinched her nipples tightly, she grinned and gave a lusty groan.

I felt her clamp down around me, and nearly lost it. I had to control myself, and it took everything I had, but I did it. I watched her, I listened, I felt every aspect of her, waiting for that moment. That moment when she was nearly on the edge.

Her nails dug into my shoulders when she leaned forward, and her pussy gripped even tighter around me. Her hips danced on me, and I couldn't stop myself anymore, I felt my own thrust up to meet her. The pain of her nails in my skin was too much like pleasure. That's when her breaths started to come in gasps and moans, that's when her back arched and she lost herself in fucking.

That's when I gave her more, that's when I drove up into her in hard thrusts that made my dragon growl within me. That's what he wanted. Oh yes, Willow's sweet pussy was pure bliss, and my dragon wanted all of it. I let him have his fill but then I took my brain back and flipped her one more time. I pulled one thigh up to tilt her just the right way and fucked into her hard and fast.

I felt her soul flit against mine for a moment and embraced even that part of her. We danced together then, our lungs about to explode, our bodies on the edge. We twined together as the pressure grew, as we both edged closer to the abyss.

"Henry..." She gasped and her hands pulled my head down to hers. Our lips fused together, and that's when the world turned a white-hot pink. I wasn't just emptying my body into hers, I was her, and she was me. Our souls fused together, and we flew apart together to become a part of the universe. This was more than plea-sure, it was Nirvana. A state of perfection, a state of oneness that only the privileged could ever reach.

We shared every aspect of ourselves in that moment. We weren't ourselves, we were something else that neither of us knew but understood totally. Then, as the moments of pleasure drew on, as the world began to contract around us once again, and we remembered to breathe, we became tiny points of moving light that pulled back together into one being, that then became two.

I found myself beside her, tangled into her, around her, completely satisfied. Nobody had ever told me about that. That was more than I'd ever dreamed possible. That was just... extra. A rueful smile played over my face and I looked over at Willow.

Her chest moved rapidly and she had her arm thrown over her face, so I couldn't see it. Her right hand was still fisted in the quilt and I saw the way her stomach rippled. She was still in the land of orgasm then. I ran a finger down the plane of her stomach and pulled back as she jolted.

"Fuck me." It wasn't a directive, but an explanation of wonder.

"Yeah. Extra." I took a deep breath and stared up at the ceiling. My head was full of her, of knowledge of her, of the things she knew and the things she didn't realize she knew. My dragon hunter, a slayer, was far more powerful than even I'd suspected.

I'm psychic, I think. I heard her in my head.

You are indeed. Plus a few other things, I answered the same way.

I can hear the thoughts of people nowhere near us. How? How do I make it stop?

Just push it away, princess. Breathe and move your thoughts from them.

I'm trying. I could feel her mentally pull away from the thoughts of her neighbors, of her mother and aunt, and smiled. Yeah, she was strong alright. It usually took psychics a lot longer to learn to control their power. *Now think of who you want to know about.*

Galen. He's happy, asleep with his parents.

Good, now, move on. No, not to me. I laughed out loud, and she clamped down on the ability.

"That's just so weird. What else can I do?" She looked at me, and I saw her own knowledge of me in her eyes.

"A few things."

"Like what?"

"You'll find out. Listen, why don't I take you to my land? We're always together here, but I'd like to show you where I'm from." I wanted to change the subject, because I didn't want to have to explain to her the ability to control light, or fire, or anything else. That was for someone else to do. Not because I didn't care, but because I did. These things were powerful tools that she didn't even know she had yet. She'd taken most things well since I'd met her, but these things, the power to take life, and maybe even give it, were things she'd need guidance with. Guidance I wasn't able to give her. She needed people who were trained to do that. I was a glorified security guard, not a teacher.

It never occurred to me that taking a newly awakened slayer for a mate wasn't a good idea. I just wanted to show her my home, my world. She could access my memories of it now, she could control what aspects of her thoughts I could see, as could I, but that was nothing like actually standing and looking at the places we considered special or sacred.

"Alright. Can we have a nap first?" She stretched, and my dragon stirred into life. So beautiful.

She was gorgeous and didn't even know it.

I let her sleep, took a shower, and woke her to have her own when I finished. She wrote a note to her mom, and then we were in the air, on the way to my home. I flew over the castle, and a little beyond it. My house was on a hill, a two-story sandstone building with as many windows as the place could take without impeding its structural integrity. I wanted to be able to see from any side of a room I was in because my land was beautiful.

I didn't fear attacks, we were the rulers of our world, after all, but I did love the splendor of the hills, the valleys, and the scenery of it all. I landed just as the sun sank, and took her into my home. I led her to the kitchen, fetched a bottle of cold white wine, and took her up to my bedroom on the second floor. We fell into bed together and I fed her sips of wine between kisses and my own sips. I wanted to be drunk on her, on the wine, and on what we'd created together.

I laughed as she giggled and took another sip of the strong dragon-made wine. Her head had already started to spin a little, but it was okay, because I'd take care of her. She got up and I followed. I wound my arms around her waist, pulled her close, and kissed her now tangy lips. She was heaven.

We sank into a slow pace of kisses, soft touches, and an exploration that lasted much longer than our first time. We didn't have that desperation now, we had satisfaction behind us, and now it was curiosity that drove us to explore. Could we recreate that fantastic spark that exploded into an entirely new world?

We spent the night in my bed, a much larger room than hers, in a much larger bed, with a thick duvet of goose down over our bodies when the night grew cold. When even that couldn't keep the cold at bay, I sparked a fire with my thoughts. The fireplace roared into life and gave us a light to explore by. I never wanted to leave my bed, or her arms.

Once more we found that Nirvana really existed, and then I slept with her in my arms. Naked and twined together, I slept peacefully for the first time in my life. I had my mate with me, there was nothing else in the world that could be better. If only we'd stayed in that bed.

Instead, I took her out into my world the next day. I took her for a walk in the hills, showed her where the fairies held their parties in the woods, took her to the lake where the selkies came out to look for mates, and then to the top of the hill where my ancestors had once ruled all of the worlds, not just mine. There was nothing there now, just a flat plain on the top of the hill where their castle once stood. I pointed out my father's castle, the place where Malcolm would rule one day, and to the other areas. The places where trolls worked farms, to the shops with elves, and the houses of the few humans we'd allowed to live amongst us.

She looked over all if it with wonder, but when she looked back at the castle, where only dragons were allowed to live, I felt tension rise inside of her. It wasn't anything she did consciously, it just happened. We walked, hand in hand, toward the place, and I felt her shoulders tense and her stomach knot. Her eyes left those of the people we passed, she stopped gasping in wonder at the flowers, fruits and vegetables, the shops, and her eyes zeroed in on the castle.

When we stepped over a drawbridge and into the castle walls, her mind went blank and I could no longer feel her soul with mine. Shit. Mary came toward us with a smile of greeting, but Willow didn't let her get close before her hand came up and blasted a pink light at my sister's feet.

People scattered as screams filled the air. Willow shrieked a terrible sound and flew at Mary. Mary, a powerful dragon in her own right, danced away. Even untrained Willow was powerful, and Mary was smart enough to sense it.

"Willow!" I shouted, totally shocked at her reaction. "Stop! That's Mary!"

I could see hatred and rage on her face. She started to tremble as she looked around frantically, her eyes searched out the exit. Guards, more dragons, came to Mary's aid, but Willow just blasted them with more of her pink light until they ran away from her.

I couldn't blame them. Swords and axes were one thing to face down, you could duck those, fight them off, but Willow's light? A strong, thick beam more like a laser that crashed into the ground with a deafening sound, was something else entirely. I could not judge the men and women that ran from Willow. I could only try to calm her down.

I reached out with my mind but found a wall of blue light blocked her from me. An angry, almost black light protected her from even me. "Willow, princess, stop, please. Nobody means you any harm here."

"I don't think she can hear you, Henry." Mary said, her hands out flat before her to show she meant Willow no harm as she moved in my direction. "We can't leave her like this. What happened?"

"I don't know, she was fine when we were in the village, the moment we stepped into the courtyard she went nuts." She was a slayer of dragons, a hunter of my kind, what did I really expect? I was so fucking stupid!

"Go to the other side, Henry. We have to stop her, or she'll kill us all."

Willow shrieked again, a blast of light split the air between Mary and me, and I dove away from the blast. I could see from her own face that she was terrified now, no longer enraged. That had been uncontrollable and far too close to me, even for her.

"Willow! That was close, my love! Stop, please!"

But she only grew more frantic and started to rain down blasts of pink light all around us. Without control now, the light came straight down from the sky, rather than from Willow's hands, and soon people screamed, fires burned, and damage was done.

Willow sank down to the ground, her knees up to hide her face, her hands over her head, and I knew she no longer had control of what happened around her, because of her. I rolled close to her, then closer, until I had her in my arms. Only then did it all stop. As she reached for me, trembling and in tears, the blasts stopped, and she hid in my arms from the world.

"Get that wretched woman out of here and don't bring her back!" I heard my father shout from above me and looked up to see his face filled with rage.

I shifted, and held Willow in my claws, close to my chest, as I flew away. I had to get her out of there, before my father could have her tortured and killed. Willow was vulnerable in those moments, her rage spent as she unleashed it in uncontrolled waves that sapped her strength. I had to take her somewhere she'd be safe, somewhere that she could learn to control what she was. But where? I flew into the world, out of my world, and into another, without a clue where to go. I had to find someone, somewhere that could help her, help us, before she destroyed us all.

7

WILLOW

Horrible images flooded my brain as I woke, and along with that came the memory of rage mingled with glee as some strange magic exploded from my hands. Screams had filled the air, a terror that had made something in me twinge with satisfaction. I'd lost my shit and, maybe, I'd killed people? Had I killed people?

No, you hurt a few, but you didn't kill anyone.

I heard Henry's tired voice in my head and turned to find him beside me. We had landed on a soft green oasis of lush grass, tall unfamiliar trees, and a stream bordered by large boulders. I had no idea where we were, but the fact that I was still alive was all that was on my mind. Did I deserve to be alive?

Of course you deserve to be alive, Willow, don't be silly.

Your dragon slayer took over, that's all. You did what you were born to do. I should have known better.

"So, I'm like an untamed animal, is that what you're saying?" I sat up and looked down at him. His eyes were a light green and strained around the edges. He was tired after a long night, my little episode, and then flying us to wherever we were.

"It's a land of fairies, Willow. Only fairies live here, but we others can sometimes come in to take a break. Nice place isn't it?" He closed his eyes and didn't bother to look around.

"It is nice, but Henry, about what happened…?" It plagued me, the knowledge that I could have killed without a second thought. I might have even killed Henry I was in such a rage.

"I know, Willow. We'll sort it, darling, I just need to rest for a little while. Only a little while." He pulled me close to his chest. His voice faded until it was little more than a whisper, and his breath became even. I settled my head onto my arm and looked around.

It was a beautiful place, but it couldn't hold my attention. I'd had a good long while to get used to the idea of magic, dragons, and fairies, even if I hadn't seen the magical worlds until recently. The place would be remarkable if I hadn't recently tried to destroy everything around me. Perhaps Arista would know what I needed to do.

I tried out my other new power, this psychic talent that had popped into life. I found her son first and saw the baby was focused on the yellow and white stripes of an umbrella. He seemed happy enough and I moved around his mind until I found his mother.

Arista... it's me, Willow. That should get her attention.

What? How did you get in my head, Willow? Stop that! She didn't sound overly pleased about my newfound ability, but then, I hadn't been too happy about it when I'd first found out Henry had been able to do the same since we met. I felt my eyes roll and sighed.

I need your help, Arista, don't make me go away just yet. Would that calm her down?

What's wrong, honey? How can I help? She sounded like she had a million questions but asked the right ones instead of the others.

I took another deep breath and thought about how to word it.

Henry took me to his world, and I sort of had a meltdown. I wasn't sure what else to say, so I went for bare minimum facts.

Oh no! Did you hurt anyone?

A little, but Henry said it wasn't bad. His father's banished me, and I'm afraid of being around any other dragons now. We kind of... I was generally a private person and not one to brag, so I didn't know how to tell her Henry had rocked my world then took me to his home, and now the world was completely different, yet again. I could barely keep up myself.

Did the deed? I could almost feel Arista's eyebrows wriggle on her face. There was even a deep chuckle of amused knowing that accompanied her question.

The connection was kind of like being on a phone, except you had your eyes closed and you heard the voice inside of your head. It was so weird to have Arista chuckle in my head, but I didn't have my phone, and even if I did, I doubted there were cell phone towers in this land of fairies.

Yeah, did the deed. That seems to have unlocked this hunting-slaying aspect of my personality. I was like Lara Croft on PCP or something. And this psychic thing of course. Henry says there's more, but I haven't had time to discover what that is yet.

Cool! And what happened with the meltdown, exactly? I could tell she'd taken a sip of a tropical flavored drink and she loved how cold and fruity it was. For a second, I could have sworn I'd even tasted the drink.

Light, lots of noisy, bangy, dangerous pink light. It was kind of awesome, but really scary too. I don't know how else to explain it other than as light. Bright, pink, and powerful.

So you can control light. Wow, that's pretty badass, cousin. Arista sounded impressed, but all I could think about was how dangerous I was.

I suppose it could be, but I need to know how to control it all, Arista. This is dangerous, me being out in public. What if it happens again and I kill somebody? I didn't like the idea of killing anyone, dragon or not. That was something else that had changed since Henry and I had mated, I still had an instinctual hatred of the dragons, but the logical part of my brain could now see past that. As long as I wasn't surrounded by dragons, that is.

Hang on, let me talk to Malcolm and find out where that place he took me is. I'm sure they can help you there. Arista disappeared from the link with my mind and it took a while, but she eventually came back with an answer.

Instead of words, or directions, she sent me a mental picture of a continent. It was large and shaped kind of like South America, but as if someone had stuck the pointy part of Africa onto the right side of it as well. Then she started to speak in my head.

Tell Henry to take you here. He won't be able to go directly to the village, but once you're in the land let me know and I'll guide you to the village where I stayed for a little while. They are a clan of dragon hunters. You can get help there.

How long will I have to be there? Now that I'd tasted what Henry had to offer me, I didn't want to be without it. The thought of being away from the anchor he was for me now was intimidating. I'd only just found what made the world make sense, now I had to let it go?

I don't know, however long it takes, Willow. Do you want to run the risk of hurting him?

That was the only question that really needed an answer, and that answer was no. I'd do whatever it took to get my powers under control and get back to Henry. I let my body relax as the sound of birds filled the air and a warm, gentle breeze played over our skin. This really was a magical land, and for a few more moments, I wanted to enjoy it with my dragon.

I was no longer his enemy, I was no longer a hunter when it came to Henry, at least. He was my mate and all I wanted. We shared a soul in two separate bodies. An odd arrangement, but that's how it was now. I was glad for the peace, so glad for the peace our mating had brought me, but I was far more grateful to have him as my mate. The man that he was now was the real Henry and I adored him.

I wanted to spend far more time with him, but it was like Arista said, did I want to run the risk of hurting him, or someone else? The unspoken but implied someone was her own husband or child. Galen was a halfling, half the child of a hunter and the other half the child of a dragon, which side would be the winner there? I'd kill myself if I ever harmed a hair on that baby's head. She was right. I had to go to this place.

First, I'd have one last nap with the man who'd broken the world and put it back together for me. I curled into him. Our bodies fit together perfectly, and the soft sound of his breath lulled me to sleep.

We woke up together, still tangled in each other, and sat up to see the sun was going down. My brain immediately went to the last image Arista sent to me, that other world, and Henry stiffened beside me.

He stood up and pulled me to my feet. "Let's find something to eat and then I'll take you there. What do you want for your last meal before I drop you off?"

I wanted a hamburger from my favorite cafe near to the town where we lived. That was my first thought. "Is there at least running water in this place?"

He looked at me doubtfully before he shook his head. "No, and no electricity either. Just you and nature. And the Amazuns of course."

"I can deal with it, but I don't know how long I can live without a decent burger. Do you think you can zap me in one every now and then?"

"Ha! You might have better luck with that than me." He pulled me close for a nuzzle at my neck before I pushed him away with a laugh.

"Can we see each other while I'm there?" I pulled at the hem of my shirt, the vulnerability in my question made me feel awkward.

"Maybe. We'll have to be very careful. They will kill me. There's more than enough of them there to get the job done."

"And you think they'll take me in?"

"You're one of them, they're kind of honor-bound to

do it." Henry scrubbed at his face with hands that touched me in all of the right places. Did we have enough time for one more romp?

"No, if I touch you now, or even think about it too long… I won't take you. Stop that, Willow!" He gave me a stern look but then ruined it with a grin. "Come on, let's feed you then get rid of you."

I laughed at the last part, I knew it was only a joke. The thought of him not being with me did hurt though, and this wasn't a trip I looked forward to.

We landed there just as night fell, after a dash back to my world for a few things, to leave a note for my mom, and to get my food. Then Henry flew like he had jet engines strapped to his wings to get me to this land of Amazuns.

We parted quietly, a last touch, a last look, a last mental promise and a kiss, and then he flew away. I was alone in a totally alien world, and I had no idea what awaited me now. I wanted to call Henry back, beg him to find another way, but I knew this was the best way. For all of us. Otherwise, I'd destroy us all.

I walked through the darkness until I came to open ground. My trainers scuffed against sand and I paused. I couldn't see much of anything yet, so I started to walk again. Lights flared into life and I realized they were torches with real flames, none of that tiki torch shit for these ladies. Oh no, this was the real deal. The torches hung from metal braces or were held aloft by women carrying them.

A long row of women came up to meet me in a rather dramatic display, and I stared at them. Dressed in unbleached cotton, not a single woman wore pants, a bra, or underwear of any kind. Some were bare-chested, others were completely naked and didn't care who saw them. It was a community of women and they'd obviously grown up in a society where they weren't taught to be ashamed of their bodies or to please men.

Around 250 women came towards me, some with small groups of girl children, others on their own. There were some with dark hair and tanned skin, others were tanned with blond or red hair. Most seemed to have black hair, including the one who wore an elaborate headdress of blue and red feathers as she came to greet me.

"Welcome, sister. You are safe here."

"Thank you. I am Willow." I didn't know what to do so I stood there with my hands in the pocket of my black sports jacket. Added to the jeans, I felt a little over-dressed and conspicuous. It was also hot here, so I wanted to take the jacket off, but I was afraid to move around too much. I'd seen a few of the women carried rather sharp and deadly looking knives.

"Thank you, Willow. I am Yohl. Your cousin came to

my sister's village not long ago, if I'm not mistaken. Arista?"

"Yes, she did. She told me about all of you." I didn't want to volunteer any more information than that.

"She is mated to a dragon. As are you." Her broad tanned face didn't judge me, it simply stated a fact.

"I am, yes." I wouldn't bother to ask how she knew, maybe she was psychic too.

"It's good you didn't lie, we can smell him on you. Come, let me show you the village and help you settle in. I suppose you want our help to train you in your powers?"

"Yes, that would be helpful, thank you." I walked up to her as she turned around. The entire village seemed to part to allow us to walk us to the center of a row of two-story huts. Each had a roof and sides made of some kind of grass, with the doorway left open. I looked at the houses as we passed and saw the doorway was a rolled-up canvas, the same grass woven into a fabric. All of the quarters contained something different, but each had a bedroom and a living space, enough for one woman, maybe a child or two. Other places in the homes held belongings and mats.

I didn't see any bathrooms or a kitchen. I'd find out why later, but for now, I settled down with my "sisters" and prepared to learn. They hadn't killed me for my dragon-taint, so maybe this would work out alright. I could only hope.

You'll get through this, Willow. I have faith in you.

Henry's voice filled my head and I stood a little straighter. I wouldn't totally be without him then.

8

HENRY

It had been a week since I'd last seen Willow, and six weeks since I'd taken her to the Amazuns. The last week had felt endless. A week of arguments with my father about "that woman", a week of bears and wolves kidnapping human women, and a week of interrogating those same bears and wolves. We had to find out who was leading this push, because they weren't doing this on their own. There was a faction in our ranks, a faction that didn't care about defying the law and it was my job to find out what I could while Malcolm was gone.

I could talk to Willow in our heads, and we'd had a few rather sexy times that would live in my memory forever because of our connection, but that wasn't enough. I could feel the weakness as it sapped my strength, a little more every day. We agreed to meet in the forest, a good distance from the village at the end of the day. I'd settled what matters I could for the day, and packed a bag. I brought her treats, the things she wanted the most from her world, and a few things I'd picked up to make the evening a little more romantic.

I'd scouted the place the day before and found the cave she'd mentioned. I landed there, unpacked the bag in my human form, and had a bottle of red wine, an assortment of chocolates, and a few other things spread out for her. I'd spread out a foam mattress on the ground, placed some fine cotton sheets on the bed, and a few pillows that had all been sealed in a vacuum bag. That had made the load much easier to carry.

I waited for her in the outfit I'd chosen based on what the women from her world seemed to find sexy for loungewear, as they called it. A loose pair of black pajama pants, a black cotton shirt with embroidered designs on it from India, and my grin. She'd have fun when she tore those buttons loose.

She was just as desperate to see me as I was to see her. I didn't just love her, I was her, and she was me, and this time apart was about to crush me. I'd never needed the presence of another person as much as I needed her, and this bond only amplified that. I spent long nights, barely asleep, trying to think of ways to please her. I'd even made several trips to check on her mother and to take her things she might need. Her mother was my family now. I'd take care of her as I would my own.

I shied away from thoughts of my own mother. That was a painful subject none of us really discussed anymore. After she'd disappeared from our lives, we all informally agreed that we wouldn't mention her anymore. It had been hard at the time, but now it was second nature to just change the direction of my thoughts.

Willow came in then, in a long panel of cotton that flowed around her hips and down her legs. It was twisted at her breasts and then tied behind her neck like a halter. The effect was sophisticated but did very little to hide her assets. Assets I wanted in my mouth and my hands.

"Come here, Willow." She'd hesitated as she came into the cave I'd lit with a few torches of my own. "I've missed you so, my darling, don't tease me now."

She had her fill of gazing at me, and fell to the bed, her lips finding mine. What followed went well beyond even our combined fantasies. Even the memory of our first time couldn't prepare us for the reality of being together once again. We made love with the hurried touches of lovers long denied contact, but with the passion and patience of long-term lovers. In the end, we were a tangled mass of legs, hair, and arms barely able to catch our breath.

"You've cut your hair," I said at last, a little sad to have missed the sensation of the silky strands against my thighs. I ran my left hand through it when she stretched out beside me on the bed.

"It kept getting in the way when I was doing the knife training, so I cut some of it off." She pulled at the length, now somewhere around the lower half of her back. "Do you hate it?"

"No, I just liked it longer. You're still you and that's what I need the most. Just you."

"Good. It will grow back, eventually." She kissed me and then sat up, her hands going for the wine and chocolate. She gave me the bottle to open and took the plastic off the chocolates.

"They have their own chocolate here, but I'm so used to mine that it tastes odd. It's good chocolate, don't get me wrong, it's just odd." She popped one of the treats into her mouth and moaned loudly. "That is so good. Orange cream, oh my God."

I smiled at her delight and watched her eat a few more. She really didn't need a lot in life to be happy. I'd grown up in splendor and wealth, my needs and desires met with a flick of my hand. She'd known poverty, hard work, and denial of even her basic needs at times. She'd gone without to make sure her mother had enough when she became older, and when she'd become ill, she'd still only thought of her mother. Where Arista had spent a fortune on doctors and insurance deductibles, Willow had seen her local doctor and hadn't gone to the specialist appointments he'd advised her to take. She couldn't afford them.

It broke my heart to know what her life had been like, what she'd given up, but in the end, the doctors couldn't help her anyway, only I could. I ran my finger down her smooth thigh and wondered how greedy she was for me tonight.

"Greedy enough for round two, dragon. Can you handle it?" She gave me a cocky smile as she popped another chocolate into her mouth.

"I can handle whatever you want to give, hunter." I liked this new aspect of her. She'd always been proud, collected, and calm, but now that edge of mistrust and anger was gone from her, replaced with self-confidence and the knowledge that she was my mate.

"You sure I won't break you?" She pushed me onto my back and I let her, too eager to feel her hot center over me to protest.

"Break me, baby, it'll be fun to have you put the pieces back together." It was a challenge and one it looked like she intended to take me up on.

Willow tested my strength after that and drove me to the brink of madness with her teasing explorations of my body, but I didn't break. I let her have her way and her fill of me. She slept after, but I stayed vigilant, keenly aware that I was in dragon hunter territory. They would smell me on her when she returned, so I'd have to leave before she did, or they'd come after me.

I knew they wouldn't punish her, she was my mate, she couldn't deny herself that, it would be suicide, but that didn't mean they had to tolerate my being here. They would control themselves, I hoped, because if they killed me, they'd kill her. My death would mean a very slow, agonizing death where she'd waste away as she was when I first met her. The hunters would not do to that to one of their own, or so I hoped.

"Only a few more weeks, I think, Henry. Then I can go home."

"You've learned so much already. Defense, how to control your psychic abilities, how to move objects around you with finesse. It's amazing really."

We didn't talk about the one thing she was here to learn though, how to control her emotions and the killing light she could produce as a weapon. That wasn't going so well.

"Has your father agreed to let me come back yet?"

"Maybe once you're done with your training I can talk him into it. Right now, no." We both sagged together. We'd have to live in her world if she didn't learn to control her light.

"I like it here, I love the women, the way they live. I mean, who knew you could use goo from tree leaves to wash your hair? They really are one with nature here. I miss my life, though. I miss my piano, my mom, and you." She paused and bit at her lip and I knew she did that to fight back tears. "I only started to like you and then we had to live apart. It sucks!"

"I know, Willow. It'll be over soon enough, I promise. You're strong, you'll figure this out." I pulled her face down to mine and kissed away the tears. "I have to leave you again, though. The sun is about to rise."

We both looked toward the mouth of the cave. There was a glow there now that hadn't been there before. The sun was coming to spoil our night. With a sigh, we both got up, packed up the bed and the other things I'd brought, and left the cave. I held her to me for the longest time, just absorbing the sensation of her pressed into me. I would miss her, I would miss how the world melted into nothing more than how she felt in my arms.

She pulled away and left quickly. I watched her go for a moment, but she didn't look back, and I knew she couldn't. If she did, I'd take her away with me and never bring her back to this place. She had to learn to control herself, so I shifted and took flight. We'd get through this, somehow.

I FLEW BACK to Willow's land and checked on her mother. I liked it there, in the peaceful quiet on top of a mountain. I could get used to a place like that. I compared her home to mine as I flew back into my own world. Willow's home was quiet, unobtrusive, meant to be a shelter from the world outside. There was certainly a quiet beauty about the place, but it was a refuge from the world, and from the elements. My home was meant to be a display of power and wealth, though I hadn't intended it to be that way.

I'd wanted a home where I could see the beauty of my own land and a place that was a defense against any threat. My home was a warning and a threat: don't fuck with me. I could see those differences now and realized Willow and I had very different mentalities. She lived in a world of peace, where war was something that happened somewhere else. My world was a place of constant vigilance to prevent wars and to be ready if it came despite those efforts.

I flew on to the castle, to find out what news I might have missed in my absence. I landed and shifted at the same time, and strode down to the room we generally used as a family meeting place. I found Arista and Malcolm there with baby Galen.

"Hello, brother, how are you?" Malcolm asked. His face was a portrait of happiness as he watched his son kick tiny legs and fists in the air from a blanket they had all settled on. I felt a pang deep in my guts as I watched them. I think it was envy, I wasn't sure, I'd never really felt that emotion before.

Malcolm and Arista touched each other often; light brushes against an arm, a face pressed against a shoulder, fingers twined together before they broke apart. That was love then, the constant need to be in contact with each other, the look of happiness they both wore as they looked down at their very own creation. I didn't want to intrude, but in our world, children were precious, and we nurtured new life together; mother, father, uncles, aunts, and cousins were all part of the village that raised a child. It was important that I spend time with my tiny nephew.

"I don't think you've held him yet, have you, Henry?" Arista pinned me to the spot with eyes that were similar, but different to Willow's. My lips parted, and my left eyebrow rose to form a protest, but she stopped me when she plucked Galen up and placed him in my hands. I wanted to snatch my hands back and refuse to take him out of fear. I'd never held a baby before.

That's why we were supposed to nurture new life. I'd never held a baby before because there had been none in my own family for a very long time. What if I broke him with my large, clumsy hands? I wanted to scream at Arista to take her son back, but Galen's tiny little head cradled into my palm like it was made for his head alone, and his little body fit along my arm perfectly. I breathed out a sigh of wonder as Arista guided my other hand to brace Galen's body and push him towards my chest.

"That's it. You won't break him, Henry. Just be gentle and make sure he's secure. Not too tight! There you go. Perfect." She smiled at me happily, but I was too busy with Galen to really notice.

His eyes had gone from that newborn blue to the crystal gray of his father, and he had the perfect blend of his parents' features. His mother's nose and high cheeks, his father's strong chin and the shape of his eyes, and his mother's brown hair. I could even see a little bit of Willow in his features and wondered if this was what our children might look like.

I ran a finger down his softy, fuzzy cheek and he opened his mouth and eyes wide. Galen's right cheek crooked just a little and it looked like he wanted to grin at me. His little fists and legs started to kick, and I had to move my hands to hold the baby securely. I turned him to face me and looked down into his little eyes. Dragon eyes. Galen was male, he could not be a hunter, but those eyes were all dragon, anyway. He would be a shifter.

"He's perfect, isn't he?" I asked quietly and looked up at the baby's parents.

"He is, but your children will be too, brother,"

Malcolm assured me. "Whatever they are when they are born, hunter, dragon, or both, they will all be perfect, because they are yours."

I could only hope he was right and that Willow and I had that chance. I knew she could do it. I knew she could gain control of her powers. I just wished it was sooner rather than later.

9

WILLOW

I hummed a song from my childhood as I toiled with the other women, a mound of corn turning into a meal in front of me as I turned one round stone over another. As I became immersed in my work, I started to sing the words to the song, totally unaware until one of the women, Nahla, poked me in the arm.

"What's up, Nahla?"

"What's this song about smoking and fucking all day that you sing? What is smoking? What is fucking?" Her beautiful face was totally innocent of mockery, and I looked at her, totally unsure of how to explain the gist of the song.

"Um, well, smoking is the act of burning a herb and inhaling the smoke into your lungs."

"Oh, like when we burn the eucalyptus leaves in our fireplaces to clear out sickness?"

"Uh, no. You roll the herbs in a paper and…" I stopped because I wasn't sure I should introduce such an unhealthy practice to these women. "Yeah, kind of like that."

"And this fucking? What is that?" She looked really interested in this part.

"Well, that's when you mate. It's a rather naughty word for it."

"Ah! I understand. And you have people that do this smoking and fucking all day? And make songs about it? This sounds like a very easy life."

"I suppose it is, yes. It's just a song, it's not really to honor anybody or anything." I had no idea how to explain the glorification of drugs and unprotected sex to a person that had no concept of my world. It would open up other topics and I had to meet Yohl when I finished with this bucket of dried corn. "I'll explain it more some other time. I have to get this done."

"Okay. But could you explain one more thing to me?" Her dark brows drew together over her eyes and I couldn't turn her down, not when she was just so curious about it all.

"Sure, honey, what do you want to know?"

"What's a hoopty? It's such an odd sounding word."

"Oh, that's like a wagon, only a very old one, you

know, the wheels won't stay on and something's always breaking on it."

"Ah. An odd choice of things to sing about." Nahla went back to her own work and I quickly finished mine.

I'd lost myself in the work and hadn't paid attention to the song I'd started to sing. I had been careful about what I did here, it wasn't that I thought the women were beneath me, but I didn't want to pollute their society with my world's problems. It wasn't always easy being here, especially when I forgot myself and said something I didn't mean to.

I cleaned the meal from the recess of the other rock and poured it into a bag made from woven grass. I tightened the straps on my grass sandals and went off in the direction of the leader's quarters. I'd been summoned, and I had a feeling I knew what it was about. I'd been with Henry again the night before, and she'd seen me coming out of the jungle. She hadn't said anything at the morning meal, but I'd felt her eyes on me. It wasn't a surprise then when one of her personal staff came to me with the summons.

I walked over the hard-packed path quickly and was soon at the entrance to her quarters. The grass panels were down on the place, and I knew this was a serious meeting. Privacy was not something needed in this community, not unless there were accusations to be made. That was the only time the panels came down on the leader's home in this temperate place where the temperature rarely fluctuated.

She'd finally decided to ask me about the dragon scent on me then. I took a deep breath and called out to the woman much taller than the other women in the village.

"Yohl? I'm here."

"Come in, Willow." Yohl came to the entrance to her quarters and pulled a panel aside. She greeted me with a smile and kind eyes.

This wasn't to be a nasty meeting then. I breathed a little easier and went in. She had dried grass mats on the floor around a bowl of the soup the villagers made from a form of carrots and onions, along with their own herbs. I sat down at the mat she indicated and took up the bowl in the customary fashion. Here, you didn't wait until something was offered, if it was at your seat then it was yours and you took it. I'd learned that my first day here when I waited for quite a long time before Yohl had figured out why I hadn't picked up my soup and explained.

"You are mated to a dragon then, Willow?" I nearly spit out my soup when she went straight to the point. Another trait of the people here. There was no beating around the bush, it was straight to the point without any kind of guile.

"I am." I'd decided all those weeks ago that if the

women were kind enough to offer me a place in their society that I'd treat them with the same respect and dignity they gave to me. There was no point in lying, they could all smell Henry on me anyway.

She watched me for a moment, her face unreadable. She was older than me, in her 40s perhaps, pretty but also very intelligent. It was her intelligence that had won her the role of leader in this village. The women voted every year to choose their leader and I'd learned Yohl had won every year for the last 20 years.

"When I was a small girl my mother took me to a village of male farmers. She'd gone to mate with one of the men there, as is our way. She also left the male infants who had been born since her last visit."

"Ah, that's where all the male babies go then."

"Yes, we don't raise them. We don't want men in our society." I understood that after seeing the harmony within the village without them around. "Anyway, one of the men caught my attention. He was tending to chickens, and I saw him kill one of the newly hatched chicks."

"Why would he do that?" I found the tale horrible but knew there had to be a reason she was telling me this story.

"He told me that the chicken had hatched with a lame leg and it would never improve. The other chickens would shun this chick, they would peck at it, until all of its feathers were gone, and they would not let it have enough food. It would starve to death after a life of being pecked at and abused. It would not have a good life and to prevent this, the farmer would take its life. He did it gently, but he still ended the lame chicken's life rather than have it live a life that only brought misery to the poor animal."

"Ah." I looked at her, unsure of what she meant. Did she think the fact I was mated to a dragon was a disability? I looked at her, but her face was blank, no answer available.

"That is all, Willow. Thank you for coming." Yohl stood up and left me then, a dismissal as good as any, but I had questions.

I stared after her, the soup forgotten. Did she think my parents should have been the same as the farmer, cruel to be kind? I couldn't wrap my head around it. I stood up and walked from the leader's quarters to my own on the edge of the village.

I'd learned a lot in my time in the village, but I still could not control my hunter. I wasn't ready to leave yet, but was that what the story meant? If I didn't leave I would be put down to save me from a life of misery? I needed far more information than the cryptic story that Yohl gave me, but she'd left me with only more questions.

I think she means that you have a choice to make yourself, darling.

A shiver passed through me as Henry intruded into my thoughts. I needed him more every time he came to me. I thought time would ease my need, that being with him would make the ache hurt just a little less, but I'd been wrong. That ache, that need, only grew worse. I fell to my knees on my own grass bed.

Henry, please, when will this end?

Yohl's words didn't matter, I didn't care what it meant, I only wanted to be with Henry. I couldn't care right now whether I had to avoid other dragons for the rest of my life, I just wanted to be with him. I'd learned to control objects, I'd learned how to pinpoint the location of others, and read their thoughts without any of them knowing it, but I had not learned how to make sure my hunter didn't go wild and kill every dragon she came across yet.

He'd only just left me that morning, but it wasn't enough. I was surviving, sure, but this life of being without him? That was cruel misery. Clarity hit me then.

Ah, you're right, my darling. You've hobbled yourself being there, you've cut off your own life. You won't learn what you need to know there. I'll be there shortly.

I sighed with relief as Henry left my thoughts. He'd be here soon enough, and this torture would be over. I couldn't learn how to control my hunter surrounded by women like me, especially women who honed their skills to kill creatures I wanted to protect. I had to leave the place that offered me sanctuary and go where I'd be confronted.

"Willow?" Yohl's voice broke into my thoughts and I looked up to see her there with a smile on her face. "You're leaving us then?"

"I am. You're right, I can't learn what I need to know here."

"True. It's a lesson you'll have to learn for your child."

"Huh?" I looked at her with confusion.

"The one you conceived a week ago. You'll hear their voice soon enough." She smiled at me gently and sat down. She held a necklace in her fingers, a fine gold chain with a rectangular stone the color of Henry's eyes wrapped in much finer gold as a pendant. "Here, take this with you. It will help you to find peace."

I took the necklace and looked at it. I didn't recognize the stone, but it was quite pretty. "Its power is to help you focus. You will need it as you continue to learn. I've never heard of a hunter that wanted to live among the dragons, but that seems to be the goal you've set for yourself. You come from a strange land, sister. I won't pretend to understand any of it, but I can try to help. I wish you many years of happiness, Willow. May you find that which you seek."

She hugged me, and I felt tears prick my eyes. "May I come back to visit?"

"Of course, you can return any time you wish." Her dark brown gaze held mine and I smiled.

"There's really a baby on the way?" I put my hand over my stomach but felt nothing.

"Yes, there is. She's going to be a strong child too. I'm not sure whether she's a shifter or a hunter yet, but she will be strong either way. I've heard her voice already, so she must be."

"A girl? Wow."

"You realize a girl child can be both, don't you? And that this might create an imbalance in the child? She may one day have to fight her very own nature, far more than even you are? Is this fair, Willow?"

Her words turned my blood to ice. I hadn't really thought about it like that. I gulped as I tried to swallow a lump in my throat. What if our passion created a child that constantly had to fight itself? I looked at her, concerned now.

"Send her here, bring her to us, and we will help her. I don't know how, but we will find a way if it's necessary."

I didn't like to have this new worry added to my list, but at least she'd been honest with me. We were playing with nature here, only I hadn't thought about it like that. I'd let the fact that Mal and Arista's son had been perfect and wonderful lull me into playing with things that could be a terrible burden for my children. Especially a girl child. My hand went back to my stomach, and I tried to seek out the tiny spark of life but found nothing yet. Would it be fair to have this child if it was going to have a life that was so mixed up?

10

HENRY

"Where are you off to now, brother? You've only just come back." Mary interrupted my thoughts as I walked down the hallway to the launch pad. The area was more a formality to let others know we were out and to keep track of who came in. Shifters could shift and fly out of a window if they wanted to, then grow larger, but father had implemented the launch pad a long time before we were even born. We'd always used it and it was habit now.

"I'm going to get Willow. She's not learning what she needs to know in that place." I spoke quickly and hoped she'd get the point. She stopped me with a hand on my arm. A delicate white hand with black-tipped nails.

"Is that wise, Henry? You know you can't bring her here if that's the case. Father won't allow it."

"I know, but this separation is unbearable and even

Yohl says she won't learn what she needs to know there. She has to be around more of our kind."

I'd spoken with Mary more than once about the land Willow was in, the things she told me about the women there, and what she'd learned. It wasn't spying, it was curiosity.

"She's from an odd land, Henry. One where the men have woven tales about how it is them that were the dragon hunters, not the women. They are so misogynistic that they can't even let the real hunters take the glory they earned. The men made the women so subjugated that the hunters don't even know who they are now. It's a strange land and I'm glad I was born here and a dragon. I'd kill somebody in that odd land of Willow and Arista's." She leaned against the wall and didn't look like she was ready to stop the conversation any time soon.

"What are you saying, Mary?" I was a little annoyed with her, it felt like she wanted to say something and wanted to work her way up to it. We weren't normally so polite or reserved with each other, and my sister's attempt to be delicate unnerved me.

"I'm trying to say that it won't be fair to drag you away from us, and she can't come here. What if you guys have children? She can't come here, and it won't be fair to raise a girl child there. It's crazy."

Anger boiled hot and liquid to the surface and I inhaled deeply to tamp it down. She meant well.

"It's not your place to worry about any child we have, Mary. We'll deal with that when and if it happens. For now, just... fuck... I don't know, try not to make things worse for us?"

I stalked away from her, shifted, and flew out of a window. I knew she meant well, but damn. Hypothetical children were something we didn't need to worry about right now. I sliced my wings through the air, dispelling my anger as I went. Mary hadn't meant any harm, but right now wasn't the time to bring up more worries.

I just wanted to reach Willow, get her back to her world, and get on with our lives together. We'd have to live separately during the day, I couldn't abandon my duties, but we could spend our nights together. We'd find a way to make it work.

My anger dissipated as I flew, it always did when I was in flight. Mary did have a point though, Willow's inner circle was female, but her world was ruled by men and catered to men. It wasn't like that in my world. Females could be, and were, just as powerful as men. We'd never had protests led by women who demanded their rights. They'd always had the same rights as men. Women didn't live to please the male gaze or to get over on other females because they didn't have to. It never entered our brains to try to subjugate females, and that would never change.

Would it be fair to raise a son or a daughter in a society that felt the son was more important because he'd been born with a penis instead of a vagina? Would it be fair to raise a daughter in a society that told her that her worth was based on her appearance and how submissive she was? I couldn't raise a daughter like that at all. I knew Willow had been raised in a matriarchal surrounding but not all people thought like that in her world.

I pondered it all as I flew, I couldn't think about anything else as I soared through the sky. We would find a way to raise our children in my world, if that was what Willow wanted, or her world, if that was what she chose. If we even had children. There was no certainty of that, after all.

Where are you? I buzzed her brain and waited for a reply. When it came, I noticed an odd tone to her voice. Something was wrong, she sounded stressed.

I'm at the cave, are you far away?

Just overhead, my dear. Are you ready? I shot down out of the sky towards her and shifted as my feet came into contact with the ground. Lush jungle and the wild cries of exotic birds went ignored. I only had eyes for my mate.

"What's wrong, Willow?" My blood raced in my

veins and my heart pounded as I looked around. I couldn't see a threat, why had she sounded so odd?

"Nothing, Henry. Let's go. I want to feel my piano keys and see my mother, and so many other things."

"Let's go then." I shifted back into a size she could climb onto and then let myself grow as I flew us into the air.

I felt a faint buzz in the area where she settled on my back. Something had her agitated and she could not settle.

Willow, tell me, what's wrong? Why are you so agitated? I can feel it buzzing through you like electricity.

I just have a lot to think about, Henry. Yohl had a few things to tell me before she let me leave. Some of it is... a lot to think about. I'll be fine. Just get me home, please.

If you promise that we'll talk once you've spent some time with your mother and settled in.

After a hot shower, too. God, I've missed running hot water. We had showers, a rather ingenious method the Amazuns thought up, but most of the time the water ran cold before you'd finish.

Oh? How would they heat the water?

With great big bowls of water left out in the sun. The water would warm during the day, and the water would flow down a bamboo pipe they'd cut in half to pour down onto you through a plate with holes in it. It worked really well, but about halfway through you'd have cold water instead of warm.

I guess you need a long hot shower after weeks of that.

I do, and my bed. They had nice little beds, but I miss my memory foam mattress so much. It's like sleeping on a cloud.

I remember. It is a rather wonderful invention.

It's heaven. And I can't wait to be in it again, so hurry up, dragon.

Her tone had changed to one of teasing now, and the stress had left it. I attributed her initial anxiety to a keen desire to return to her home, and flew on. I added extra beats to my wings to pick up the pace and we soared like a rocket through the sky. It was dark in her world when we landed, and Willow ran into the house of her mother before I could even blink.

She was glad to be home then. Her mother already had food in the microwave and a mug of tea in front of Willow by the time I made it into the house. She beamed at me and handed me my own mug.

"Thank you for bringing her home, Henry. I sure have missed my baby girl." Rachel was beaming brightly, her naturally thin frame covered in a pair of loose jeans and blue and black plaid flannel shirt. Her hair, dark but graying at the roots, was just as long as Willow's had been before her trip and trailed down her back in a thick wave.

"I'm glad to bring her back to you, Rachel. She's

missed you."

"I still can't wrap my head around the whole time thing. She's been gone for months, but it's only been a few weeks in that world?"

"Yes, time passes much slower in that place."

Willow piped up to offer an explanation. I was glad she did because her mother seemed to accept the answers she gave without further questions.

"Well, whatever it takes to keep you happy and healthy, baby. Do you want cornbread with this? I can heat some up." She put a bowl of some kind of brown beans in front of Willow.

"Cold is fine, Momma." Willow grabbed a piece of the bread and crumbled it into the beans to make a mush. It didn't look like the most appetizing food in the world, but the smell and the way Willow shoveled it into her mouth said it must be delightful. I'd try it one day, when I was hungry. For now, I watched her eat happily.

"I'll, uh, head on over to Eve's in a little bit. I'm sure you two want to be alone." Rachel stood up and went to her room to grab some things before she went over to her sister's house. Arista's mother didn't live far away, and Rachel insisted so I didn't protest. I remembered the memory foam mattress Willow had spoken about. It was rather heavenly.

Rachel soon left us to our own devices and Willow hopped in the shower. She was gone for a long time and

I decided to make a pot of coffee instead of interrupting her moment of shower-fueled bliss. When she came into the kitchen her hair was damp, her face was wreathed in smiles, and she had the fluffiest white robe I'd ever seen. I sat down the dregs of my first cup, turned the pot off, and crossed my arms as she grinned at me.

She came up to me, her eyes sparkling with twinkles, and pressed her lips to mine in a kiss meant to tease. Her lips were warm and soft, smooth, and she tasted of toothpaste. I'd tasted the cinnamon on her lips when my tongue darted out to lick her lower lip.

Her mouth opened and her tongue tangled with mine in the slow perfection we'd both settled on long ago. Slow, long licks that teased each of us with tawdry ideas of what else we could do with our tongues. My hand came up to caress her cheek as we kissed. I'd wanted her for my entire life, even before I knew her, I think. She was perfection to me, no matter what flaws she thought she had.

I backed her into a wall, and the belt on her robe fell open as she moved. Our lips clung together as we moved. We spent a little time relearning each other's taste with languid licks that dragged out the pleasure the moment of freedom without worry about interruptions.

Her hands fluttered to my waist, as if she was not sure of where she wanted to touch me first. They moved, came around to my chest, then along my neck, before they settled on my shoulder blades. She wanted me close, she'd decided. I moaned into her lips as I felt her breasts press into my chest.

"Are you sure you want to do this in your mom's kitchen and not the bedroom, princess?" I slanted my lips down her cheek and over her neck, to that spot that stole her breath away when I nipped at it. She loved that spot and what it did to her, so I knew when I blew on it that I'd get a reaction. Her knees went weak and she sighed in pure happiness.

"I don't care where you fuck me, Henry, so long as you fuck me, baby." Her light brown eyes drilled into mine and I grinned.

"After so many nights in a cave, my love, I think a nice, proper bedroom would make a rather wonderful change," I said before I pulled Willow in the direction of her bedroom.

"Your wish is my command, Henry," she responded, and followed along behind me eagerly.

"I somehow doubt that, princess, but I'll take that answer for now." I kicked the door shut as she came through it and pushed her down to the bed with just enough force that she grinned at the motion. She bit her lip in an eager way, a way she only did when she was contemplating something especially naughty.

"You're the one in control, my love. Show me what you want from me."

She sprawled there on the bed, her legs open and her feet planted on the edge of the bed frame. Her stomach had grown flatter over the weeks as she toiled with the Amazuns, and her legs were shapely and tanned now. All of her was tanned, as a matter of fact.

"How much time did you spend naked at that place, exactly?" I looked over the beautiful canvas of her skin, the delicate ridges of her ribs, down her abdomen, to the very center of her that I wanted to taste so very much. I bent down to my knees in front of her and parted her thighs a little wider.

"Oh, I only put clothes on when you came to visit." She spoke with a breathless giggle and I knew she was breathless because she anticipated the feel of my tongue in her hot folds.

"But you only took them off again as soon as you came into the cave. So you must have been naked every hour of the day." That made me harder than I thought it would. I liked the idea of Willow nude, comfortable, and carefree.

She shook out her length of light brown hair, and I felt my hands clutch together. I so wanted to get my hands in those silky strands, wrap them in my fist as I guided her mouth over me, up and down, and fuck, I'd blow if I didn't stop it. She had learned some skill at taking my dick in her mouth, and she sucked me as sweetly as I knew she would.

For now, I wanted to taste her more than I wanted her to taste me.

I was about to swipe at her with my tongue when she sat up, let the robe fall from her shoulders, and placed her hand over the hard bulge in my pants. She must have changed her mind about who was in control because she looked up into my eyes with a seductive glance before they fell down to my pants again. She pulled the belt loose before she unbuttoned my pants. Her tongue snaked out to wet her now dry lips and I knew she was as eager as I was for what came next.

Oh, so eager.

I kicked my boots and socks away before I let my pants fall to my feet.

I was barely breathing by the time she wrapped her delicate fingers around me and grinned up at me with a wanton smile. She licked me from the base of my dick, all the way to the super-sensitive tip. I nearly rocked back out of her hand when her lips wrapped around me. I looked down and realized how huge I looked in her hand, how small her mouth was when she began to swallow every single hard inch of me.

I watched, my breath held as the thick rope of my dick disappeared between her luscious lips and down the back of her throat.

When she sucked her way back up my shaft I let my head fall back and gave a groan that felt like it came from the tips of my toes. She sucked at my cock with her cheeks and made my world rock on its axis when she swiped at me with her sweet little tongue.

My hands were soon buried in her hair, to guide her exquisite movements.

My moans grew louder and groans slipped from between my gritted teeth as she sucked at me. "Fucking hell, Willow. You suck my dick so fucking good!"

I have to admit, by this point, I'd forgotten I wanted to eat her pussy until she screamed my name, because all I wanted to do was come straight down her tight throat. She made it even harder to hold back when she swallowed every inch of my cock that she could.

"Fuck, Willow, stop. Princess, please, you have to stop. I'm going to come in your mouth if you don't!" I pulled at her hair gently, tried to move her face away from my painfully hard dick, which was its own torture, but she only paused for a second to look up at me with a cheeky little grin.

"We have time, baby, it's not like you won't be hard again in five minutes, anyway." Her words had made me groan in anticipation before she sucked my hard flesh into her mouth again.

I cupped her face gently while her lips and throat worked me into a state I could not turn back from. It felt selfish, but I couldn't help but love it.

Sex with Willow was mind-blowing because we

eventually came together as one soul, but when we focused on giving the other an orgasm and didn't join together, it was a whole different world. An orgasm times a million. She'd get her own back, as she predicted, within five minutes anyway. I didn't play around.

She moaned, and the vibration went up my shaft, straight to my balls, and before I could warn her, the first drop of my essence had landed on her tongue.

"Fuck… Willow," I ground out as she swallowed the last drop, so greedy she left no traces of what she'd done anywhere.

She gave me enough time to catch my breath before she pulled me down to kiss me.

I pulled her up to my mouth and kissed her deeply. She pushed me down to the bed.

She straddled my waist, her eyes hungry to look at every inch of me, followed by fingers that teased and skimmed all the sensitive places she'd discovered I had. Her lips prolonged the tease with kisses that lingered, or a stroke of her tongue against silky skin. My hands wound in her hair again, a rope between us that I fed out as she trailed down the length of me. Her eyes, oh her eyes nearly made my heart burst with all the emotion they contained. She made promises with those eyes, promises about the future, about her love, and about right now. The only moment that really mattered out of them all.

It was well past time I gave her what she gave to me, and I rolled over to drop her on the bed beneath me. My legs straddled her slender hips, and I gave her the same slow exploration that she'd given me. I felt my dick press into her abdomen, a soft resistance that was its own pleasure, but ignored the temptation to just slip into her. I wanted my mate to be incoherent with need when I slid into her.

I took in her flesh with my eyes, then kissed my way down her neck before I pulled away to look at the breasts that had always overfilled my hands. They seemed, somehow bigger than they had only hours before but perhaps that was just my imagination. I didn't imagine her response as I grazed the wet tip of my tongue on her right nipple.

Her hips surged up into me, and her eyes went wide. They were glazed with lust, those beautiful brown eyes of hers. I teased one dark tip and then the other with a long, hard suck in the wet heat of my mouth. Her hips began to twist beneath me with each tug of my lips, and I chuckled quietly under my breath. She loved it when I teased her.

My hands stroked a path down her ribs, over her stomach, and down into the naked temptation that was so sweetly responsive. I felt her body buck beneath me as pleasure burned through her. My questing fingers found her clit and that's when our souls began to feather around each other.

I felt her pleasure as my own, in places that still felt new and wonderful to me. A woman's pleasure felt different to a man's and from past experience, I learned that the orgasm wasn't the only part of sex that could be good for a woman. The getting to it could be just as much fun, in its own way.

I tugged a little harder at her nipple, to the point of pain but not over that threshold, when my fingers slid into her. I opened her gently with two fingers, and her slick walls grasped at me in a ripple of delight, so I tugged a little harder on her nipple.

"Henry…" she gasped my name in a way that made my rock-hard body *throb* in response. I loved the way she panted my name. It was so needy, so sweet, so sexual.

I rearranged my hand so my thumb pressed into the sensitive button of her clit tightly, just the way she liked. Willow didn't want soft and delicate, she wanted to know she was being pleasured, she wanted to *feel* my touch on her. She'd never get off with soft kisses and butterfly touches, not my mate. She had to know I'd been there.

"My little savage," I said with her nipple between my teeth. "So fucking savage."

Her nails raked down my back as I spoke, and I felt her pleasure start to bloom. I wasn't a part of her, at that point, but I was a part of her pleasure. I felt the way her walls clenched and rippled around my fingers in my own groin, I felt the way her muscles tensed from her toes to the top of her head, and then exploded in rippling waves. My own breath exploded from me when hers did, and she screamed my name.

I rode the waves with her, higher, and then higher, and lost all sense of space and time as she found a dark place where only pleasure existed. We floated there, me tied to her through our spirits, until we came back to the real world.

I caught my breath beside of her and watched her face. I knew she wasn't quite finished yet and grinned when her eyes came open.

"We aren't done yet, right?" she asked with a slow smile.

I looked down at the evidence of my desire to carry on, and looked up to see her eyes were in the same place.

"No, I don't think we are, do you?"

"Not at all, Henry. Come here." She rolled over to find my lips with hers; a sweet kiss that soon turned into so much more.

She didn't just straddle me and get on with it, she took her time, and built us both back up.

"I've waited so long to have this kind of freedom

with you," she said softly, her lips just below my ear. I inhaled the scent of her hair as my fingers wound through it. I never wanted this time together to end.

She moved then, her passion aroused once more as she touched my skin. I could feel her heat between us, wet and hot, and so ready to take what I had to give. She sank down onto me, and her back arched as she sank halfway down. She paused, her delicate internal muscles squeezing to make me shiver as she looked right into me.

"I never want this to end," she whispered as she took the final inches of me into her. She waited for a moment to let her body adjust to me all over again, and then she started to move. Those sweet, subtle hitches that soon turned into a keening cry, a wild ride, and the sensation of leaving my body to join with hers.

"I'll never let it end, Willow," I promised as she bottomed out on my dick, every centimeter of her pussy full of me.

She moved against me and my hands tightened on her hips as she looked down at me. Her eyes caught on my parted lips and she traced their outline with a finger I soon sucked between my lips, an imitation of what we did much lower.

Willow gasped, and her pussy went tight around me, a perfect glove for my thick dick.

She moved on me with experience now, an expert in

how to massage me straight to the place she wanted me to be. I moved my hands over her breasts, to flatten them in my palms. Her left hand came up to cover mine as her right hand pulled away from my mouth. I watched as the finger that had left my mouth now moved down between her thighs, to the liquid smooth velvet of her clit. My fingers clamped down on her nipples as she moved her hips and ground her clit into her finger while she fucked herself on my dick.

My shy but curious little princess had turned into a wanton vixen and I loved every minute of it.

My body responded to the gasped sighs she let go and my dick grew even harder. It was too late to fight it now, I'd waited for this moment for too long. I felt her nails dig into my chest as her left hand grasped at me, and I responded with a desperate thrust into her wet heat.

"That's it, Henry. Come with me, baby. Come with me," she urged me to follow her as my hands dropped down her waist, one going to her hair, the other clutched onto her ass. My hand clenched at her ass, massaged it and guided her movements before I sought out a part of her that was deeper, pushing between the globes of her ass to find the dark little secret that hid there. Willow gasped above me and clenched on top of me as my middle finger teased at the entrance. I wondered if she'd be brave enough, what it would feel like, to get inside of her *there*.

"What are you doing?" she panted, and I felt my eyes widen and my lips spread in a grin.

"Finding out what makes you come the hardest, princess, what else?"

Her only response was a garbled moan as the tip of my finger teased at her there. Her back arched as my finger slowly slid into the tight passage, just enough to let her feel the invasion. The response was immediate and noticeable as she started to come apart around me.

My dick surged as she cried out my name and her sweet little pussy tried to swallow me. I groaned as the first hot jet of me filled her, and then our souls danced together, fused just along the edges. This time, when we found each other, we became one, our bodies abandoned as we merged into a single soul, and forgot the world existed.

Her leg clenched around me, and I pulled her head down to invade her mouth with my kiss. Her nails raked at my skin as she writhed above me in my arms, all mine, body and soul. I worked my hips to thrust up into her, I knew she came a lot harder when I did that, and so I pushed up into her, deep and hard.

I looked into her eyes as we fucked, as we fused, and sucked on her bottom lip. She was mine and I was hers, and that was all that mattered.

11

WILLOW

"This is beautiful!" I heard my mother say as we drove up to the house I now owned a week later.

"It will be once everything's in place." I smiled at her happily. "We won't always be here, Henry still has duties in his own world, but this will be my home from now on."

Just like my aunt and my mother, I'd chosen a house on top of a tall mountain, accessible by a dirt road only. It was two stories of dark-stained log cabin that blended perfectly into the background. A wide porch, braced by wide beams into the side of the mountain, overlooked the valley below. It sat perfectly to catch the morning sunlight with the large panes of glass that served as walls. Henry had found it online, when he'd discovered how to use my computer, and showed it to me. He knew it was the one I'd want, and he'd been right.

Money appeared for the transaction through a company his world had set up a long time ago and a deed was brought to me by courier a few days later. Now I had the keys, and I'd driven Mom up in the new car Henry had also provided for me.

"He's coming by later, but he had to get some work done this morning. Come on, let me show you around." I grinned at her as I turned the engine off and we climbed out to head up the steps of the back of the house. We walked into a large room; smaller rooms branch off it to one side. The first floor had the long and wide living room, a kitchen to the right, a staircase on each side, and a full bathroom on the left. Upstairs there were six bedrooms, a bathroom, and a room I was going to use as my music room.

I beamed as Mom gasped and looked around at all of the space. "Oh honey, he's done right by you."

"I think so." The furniture was due to arrive the next day and we'd planned to set it all up together, but I couldn't wait to show Mom.

"It's just beautiful." She walked around the room, her steps a hollow sound in the now empty space. "I can't believe it. It's so beautiful."

"Thanks, Mom. Look, over there on top of that hill?

That's your house. I can wave at you from here." I pointed off into the distance and she laughed.

"Oh honey, I'd never see you with these old eyes of mine. I'll have to get a telescope to see you wave."

I felt a pang at her words. Except for the time I'd spent at the university, we'd never really been apart. I'd always lived with my mother, and we'd taken care of each other over the years. "You know you're always welcome to come here and live with me? There will be many nights when I'm alone here."

"Oh, Willow, no, baby! You need to settle in with Henry and get used to each other. Neither one of you needs me underfoot as you make that adjustment." She patted my cheek and wandered off to the stairs to the left of the house. That's where my piano would go.

"Henry's ordered a new piano for me. I told him my old one was fine, but he wants to hear me play a grand piano." I smiled when her eyes went wide.

"He's good to you, baby. Don't ever doubt that."

I didn't, and when we walked into the room, I had even more proof of how good he was. Black lacquered, highly polished wood greeted us, set up in the perfect place. The piano was luxurious, beautiful, and more than I could have dreamed of. Henry sat behind it on the bench, a grin of expectation lighting up his eyes.

"Well?" he asked, his eyes on me.

"It's beautiful, Henry!" I let my fingers dance on the piano, memorizing its shape as I moved along.

"Rachel, I have a question," Henry piped up and I turned to him. What did he want to ask my mother?

"I know Willow's father isn't the picture, so I won't worry about him, but you're present and a huge part of her life. I feel it's only right, to do all of this right. I've learned that it is your custom to ask for permission to marry, so, if you would do me the honor, may I please make Willow my wife in every way?"

"Seems to me you've done that part, already." Mom had the audacity to snicker and she laughed even harder when she saw my shocked face. "Look at her face! Of course you do, you silly man. Imagine such a thing!"

I didn't know which of them had shocked me more, Mom or Henry.

"Willow? Princess?" Henry had to snap his fingers to get my attention. I was still stunned, and my jaw dropped a little bit more when he bent in front of me and took out a ring box.

He opened it to reveal a delicate, dragon-made ring of gold, diamonds, and a large, centered, square-cut emerald, between the band of diamonds. "Willow, will you marry me?"

It was every schoolgirl fantasy I'd ever had come true! I stared down into Henry's eyes and forgot how to breathe. "Uh..."

I couldn't make words, I couldn't even shake my head, all I could do was try to blink away tears as the man who was now my best friend, my literal soul-mate, and the man of my dreams asked me to be his wife. I finally sank down to my knees with him and kissed him.

That started my brain again, and I whispered yes to him over and over again. Mom gave a whoop of delight and ran out of the room. She was calling Aunt Eve, if I knew her at all. Henry stood up and pulled me against his body. His kiss was one of happiness, not passion, and his smile was infectious when I pulled away.

"Put me down, silly!" I laughed, and he put his hand over my stomach as he followed my command.

"Can you hear her yet?" We'd both been waiting for the voice of our child to become real to us.

"Not yet, but I guess it will happen. Arista said it happened with her. Galen turned out to be a boy, though, do you think that's the difference?"

"Could be. If she's pure hunter with none of my dragon aspects, that might be why."

"You're right. So, when do you want to get married?" I waited expectantly, thinking it would have to be soon if I wanted to find a dress that wasn't huge so it would fit over my belly.

"This weekend?" he looked eager and I couldn't say no.

"That's way too fast, but why wait?" I gulped a little.

A few days to find a dress and have a wedding, oh that was going to be fun.

"Exactly. There's no need for it. It will be a test too, to see how you react to more dragons around you now."

"It went okay at Mal and Arista's wedding..." I hadn't developed my full powers at that point, though.

I'd had time to heal, become used to my powers, and learn how to focus them since then. It could prove dangerous.

"We'll just measure how you feel as each one arrives. My father will be here, my brothers and sisters, and a few other dragons in my extended family. When you reach a point where you think you can't handle it, we'll start to turn guests away."

"I knew you were a smart man, Henry." I leaned over to peck his cheek and sat down at my piano. I began to play for him, the first song on my brand-new piano. It had been tuned perfectly and was in just the right position to catch sunlight and moonlight, throughout the day.

I'd started out hating this man, this dragon, but now I couldn't imagine life without him. It wasn't just the awesome sex, the gifts, or the fact he was gorgeous as sin. It was that he was generous, he made me laugh, he lifted me up, and he let me into his own world. We were one in spirit, definitely, but we'd also become really good friends, and that's what mattered.

You could have the man of your dreams but if you couldn't have a good time together, or you just went places with him to make him look good, or if you only liked to have sex with him and not do the things he liked to do, it wouldn't work. You had to have separate hobbies, of course, but you had to have some kind of common ground, otherwise it wasn't really a relationship.

Now, I was about to be a wife, a mother, and a best friend. To a dragon. The music I chose, a piece I'd composed myself, sank into a darker melody as my fingers pressed into the keys with more weight. I'd panic about my future if it wasn't so brilliant looking. I'd planned a life of music and nothing more, but Henry had changed those plans. He'd given me a different direction to go into, while supporting my original goal at the same time.

The notes became lighter, happier, as my thoughts changed, and Henry and my mother, back from her phone call, both beamed at me with pride. Six months ago, I thought I'd be dead by now. I thought I'd have withered away to nothing, with nothing to show for the life I'd lived, except for a few pieces of music I'd composed. How my life had changed when Henry showed up with Malcolm.

I closed my eyes and let myself fall into the music. It flowed from my brain, down my arms, and into my fingertips, each note memorized, executed perfectly now.

It's beautiful, Willow. I opened my eyes and looked around. I didn't recognize the childish voice.

Who is that? I thought, perhaps, I'd wandered off into a psychic connection, but I hadn't. I was in for another shock.

It's your daughter, Willow. You'll name me Marya when I'm born, or so I'm told.

Marya? I wasn't sure I liked the name, but if she said that was her name, then so be it.

Yes, Marya. Please don't stop playing, Willow. It's beautiful, this music you play.

Henry! I looked up at him to see he'd heard it too. Our baby was alive and well. And quite precocious for her age, I thought with a grin.

I played another piece, a different composer, until the baby went back to sleep, or whatever it did. I stopped being aware of her after a while but kept playing until I was too tired to play anything else.

"Let's go find something for dinner, Willow." Henry came to lift me from the piano bench and I didn't think the world could be any better than it was now.

Maybe it was pregnancy hormones, maybe it was just months of ceaseless upheaval, but in this moment, the world was perfect. I didn't have to say the words,

Henry saw it in my eyes. I loved him, for all that he was, despite our bond, not just because of it.

If Arista was this happy, then we both had far more out of life than we'd expected to get.

"Your mother is waiting for us." I knew the rest of the sentence was, "or I'd fuck you crazy on that piano."

"We have time, Henry, we have time." I patted his cheek and then we went downstairs.

I'd have to call Edana, I thought as I drove us off of the mountain. "Mom, do you know how to contact Edana?"

"Your cousin?" Mom asked, as if she wasn't certain about who I meant.

"Yeah, I think she was. She used to babysit Arista and me when we were little."

"I think Eve might know how to contact her. I'll find out. Do you want her to come to the wedding?"

"She was the first one that told us about veils and special dresses, and she used to bring dresses she'd made from old pillowcases for us to play wedding day in. Yeah, I would like to invite her."

"Then we'll find her for you, baby." Mom patted my arm from the back seat.

"You know, if you can handle it, we'll have to have a dragon wedding too?"

I almost hit the brakes with that one. "Pardon?"

My eyes were wide and I could feel how high my left eyebrow had arched.

"Father will want it, as will the elders. Malcolm and Arista are planning theirs already." Henry sounded like he wasn't any happier than I was about the prospect.

"We'll figure it out, Henry, don't worry." I patted his hand and tried to concentrate on the dirt road filled with sharp rocks that had been weathered from the ground.

"I hope so. We can do without it if we have to, but it would be nice, just to keep those in my world happy. I'm third in line, now that Galen's come along, so I still have to follow some of the traditions."

"We'll sort it, I don't know how, but we'll get through it, Henry. That's what it's all about, isn't it? Having each other to get through the good and the bad times together." I gave him what I hoped was a brave smile, but inside I felt panicked. A wedding in an entire world full of dragons? It might be the end of me!

12

WILLOW

We pushed the wedding back two weeks, it was impossible to do it any sooner with the schedules we all had, and Edana wasn't going to be available until that weekend anyway. We'd spent that time on the house, on the preparations for the wedding at our home, and on each other. Henry still had to go to his world for most of his day, but we looked at it as no different to a commute other couples lived with.

He just happened to be a dragon who made a daily commute between two worlds. We spent our nights together, and some of our days, when he could be away. There was something going on in his world. He didn't talk to me about it much but he'd told me some of it. Human women had been kidnapped and taken to his world to be the mates of wolves and bear shifters. I knew he felt a heavy weight over it all, but he didn't want to burden me with it.

I understood and didn't push. It was none of my business really. I focused on where furniture should be placed, which dress to buy, and which flowers needed to be planted around the house. I liked my world the way it was and didn't really want that to change. It kept my mind off the disaster our wedding might be if I lost my control and started to zap our guests.

Edana turned up the day before the wedding and drove up to the house in a black SUV with tinted windows that were probably illegal they were so dark. She stepped out of the car. A tailored gray linen suit accentuated her curves, and I felt memories flood my brain. She'd been so protective of Arista and me, so full of excitement about her future, and then when she'd turned 18, she'd disappeared. Her family was gone, and with only distant relatives around, she'd taken a training opportunity in the city and left us all behind.

I didn't really know a lot about her life after she'd left us but hoped to find out more. She was a beautiful woman, with similar features to the rest of the females in the family. The main exception was her eyes. Where most of us had some shade of brown or green, Edana's eyes were a crystal-clear gray. They were almost color-less, a fact that startled me when I first saw them again. I'd forgotten how clear they were.

I went down the steps of my new home, a slight bulge already starting around my tummy, and felt some new emotion overtake me. It was like I'd found a long-lost sister after decades of separation.

"You haven't changed a bit, Edana!" I was amazed at just how youthful she looked. You'd never guess she was thirteen years older than me, or that seventeen years had passed since I'd last saw her. She didn't even have those fine lines around her eyes that women started to get after the age of thirty, or any of the little telltale signs that she'd aged. She was tall, with a little extra weight around her hips, but otherwise appeared to be quite fit.

"You have, little girl! Wow, look at you! What a beautiful woman you turned into!" She embraced me, a wide smile on her rose-colored lips.

"You're being kind! Come in, let me show you around!" I led her into the house and to the kitchen. "Do you want a drink, something to eat?"

"A drink of some kind would be nice, thanks, Willow. What a beautiful house!" Her eyes took it all in, those exotic looking eyes, and I couldn't believe she was real.

"I have wine or soda, tea, water, milk?" I listed things until she heard one she liked, and then I handed her a small bottle of apple juice with a glass. She left the glass and took a sip of the juice before she spoke again.

"So, this fella of yours, is he some kind of drug dealer

or something?" I knew it was a joke, and I laughed with her.

"No, he just inherited his money." It wasn't really a lie, and I preferred to stay on the side of honesty, at least with my family. Edana was a distant cousin, after all.

"Always the best way to make it. When do I get to meet him?" We walked into the living room and she went to stand at the glass wall. It always took my breath away. I bent over to look through the telescope in the direction of Mom's house. Henry was going to bring her over later when he came home.

"Later, he's at work right now."

"He works?" She seemed curious about that, and I knew she was the inquisitive kind.

"Yeah, he and his brothers run a security agency." Another almost-truth.

"Cool. This is really great, Willow. I'm glad your mom tracked me down. I've always wondered what happened to you two girls."

"We always wondered what happened to you too. It was odd how you left." I was about to ask her more about that, but she shied away from the subject.

"Yeah, an opportunity came along that I couldn't turn down. I didn't want to spend my life up in these hills, where I'd likely end up barefoot, pregnant, and dead, like my mom, so I left when I had the chance." She spoke brusquely, as if she wanted to get away from that line of conversation.

I found her a little hard on the edges, as if she had a lot to hide, a lot of hurt inside of her that made her standoffish. Her mother had died when she was tiny, and none of us knew a thing about her father. She'd been raised by her grandmother until that poor woman died too, and so Edana hadn't had any reason to stay when opportunity knocked. I couldn't blame her for leaving. Her words about our area were true, but that didn't mean there still wasn't a little bit of sting that came with them.

"You seem to have done alright for yourself." I wanted to defuse the situation, so I went to the black leather couch and sat down.

"I have, I guess. It took a while, and a lot of fighting, but I manage okay, now."

"What do you do?" I put my hand up to my head to prop it up, my elbow on the arm of the couch. I was relaxed and wanted to encourage her to do the same. She seemed tense, even when she wanted me to think she wasn't. I was too observant not to notice it though.

"I work with the government. Justice sort of stuff. Where are you having the ceremony?" Again with the subject change. Interesting. She had a lot to hide it seemed. Maybe it was her job to be evasive about so much. Then again, maybe it was just that she barely knew me now and wasn't the kind to be all girly and share her entire life with people she barely remembered.

"Over in the back, there's a kind of glen there, you know the kind of place, they're common enough here. We wanted to get married where we planned to spend our lives together." I volunteered the information in the hopes it would help her to open up a little. It didn't.

"That sounds really great. I'll go get my things, shall I?" She was going to stay here at the house with us and keep an eye on it for us while we spent two days in another world, one without dragons.

I decided that my old babysitter might be a little bit odd, but I was still glad I'd invited her to the wedding. Beneath that calm exterior, I knew she had secrets and probably a lot of hurt that she wanted to hide. I'd let her have her secrets, for now.

Arista... I sent out a message to my cousin and wasn't surprised when she answered back immediately.

What's up, sweet thing? She'd become fond of giving us all endearments lately, and it had rubbed off on me to an extent. We were both happy, why shouldn't we let the world know it?

I'm not sure Edana knows anything about what we are. I rushed to inform her, not certain of how long I had before Edana came back.

It wouldn't surprise me, honey. We thought Mom was

kooky for the longest time. Why should Edana know any different than we did?

You're right. Okay, she's coming back, I'll invade you again later. I heard her laugh darkly as I cut the connection between us and shook my head. I knew that last part would make her laugh, but that laugh was so wicked it made me grin.

"I'll show you up to your room." I led Edana upstairs, on the opposite side of the house from our room. I wasn't sure yet whether we'd reveal any of the truth to her, so I'd put her on the far side so she wouldn't overhear anything if we talked. Henry's side of the family knew my side weren't all aware of their true natures so they'd all agreed to arrive by car. Even if that car only came from halfway down the mountain.

I left Edana to settle in and went downstairs to look out at the scenery. Something had bugged me about Edana, but I couldn't put my finger on it.

I jumped when a knock came at the door. I'd been so lost in my own thoughts that I hadn't noticed a car approaching. It must be someone Henry sent. Henry wouldn't knock. I wasn't surprised to find Henry's brother, Aleric, on the wide back porch, his face a little sheepish. When he wasn't around me he was a soldier through and through, but if he came anywhere near Arista or me, he turned into a shy little boy.

"Hi, Willow. Henry sent me to bring you these." They

were cut flowers from his world. Bright peach and purple blooms filled his arms and I took them as I held the door open for him.

"Thanks, sweetie. Come on in. Let me get you something to drink." He loved my sweet iced tea, so I took him into the kitchen to get him a glass and to put the flowers in a special fridge we'd bought for the wedding foliage.

"Willow, I—"

I turned to see Edana come into the kitchen. Her words stopped as she spotted Aleric. All six-foot-four-inches, blond-haired and blue-eyed god of a man, Aleric. And he was god-like, Henry's youngest brother. So god-like Edana just stared at him as if she'd been smacked in the back of the head with a board. "Uhmmmmm…"

I glanced at Aleric, immune to his charm because I was his brother's mate and saw the same expression on his face. Oh damn. I waved a hand between them, but neither even blinked as my hand waved around. Instead, they moved closer together.

Yep, they were mates if I knew anything about it. I heard shocked inhalations as each reached out to touch the other, and decided it was time for me to vacate the premises. I didn't want to witness whatever came next, even if both were beautiful examples of their species. I felt a giggle rise in my chest and left the room, the quiet "hi" that came from Edana finally broke me and I ran to my bedroom to laugh into my pillow.

That hadn't been exactly what happened with Henry and me, so it was amazing, but I thought they'd prefer to have a private moment together. Whether she knew it or not, Edana was a hunter, and she was mated to a dragon. The cycle was about to begin all over again. Only this time, it seemed there was an attraction there that definitely negated the hunter part of me that had repulsed me from Henry at first.

Willow, you shouldn't laugh. I think it's sweet!

Oh, baby, little dumpling in my oven, it is sweet. I'm not laughing to be mean, I'm laughing because I'm delighted.

Hmm, are you sure?

Of course I'm sure, dumpling. Momma isn't cruel, you know?

No, I know you aren't, Willow. He is very handsome, isn't he, Uncle Aleric?

Yes, he is, dumpling. She's a very lucky woman.

She's much older than him.

Not really, six years I think.

That's an entire generation in your world.

Yes, but he's a dragon, sweetheart, they age differently anyway.

That's true. Do you think Grandfather can take another son being mated to a hunter?

He'll just have to get used to it. It's happening for a reason after all, isn't it? Fate or whatever has chosen this path for all of us. It's not like we chose to be mated to each other.

I suspect you're right, Willow. I'm going to nap now. Goodbye.

The baby was a bit officious sometimes, far too precocious for her own good, and I had to wonder what she'd be like once she was born. Arista had said the bond had gone after Galen was born. Her psychic powers weren't as strong as mine, and the only reason I could communicate with her that way was because of my own abilities. I hoped the bond between Marya and I continued after she was born, I'd come to cherish those moments with her. Even if she did sound rather like a 90-year-old woman that stood in judgment of her own child, not a child speaking to their parent.

I patted the spot where I thought Marya would be busy doing her growing and judging, and waited to hear something from downstairs. Not too loudly though, from the look of the pair, I might not want to hear whatever might happen down there. Henry sent me a warning a few minutes later. He was on his way in.

I told him to land in the trees and made a lot of noise when I went down the stairs. I didn't care what they were doing, I just didn't want to see anything. I was surprised to find them still stood together, they hadn't moved at all.

"Hey, can either of you hear me now?" They snapped

apart, and I grinned. "People are going to show up soon, get yourselves together. We have a glen to decorate, plans to finalize, and stuff to do. If you're helping, get to it. Otherwise, there's fresh sheets on your bed, Edana, and you have your own bathroom on that side."

I went out to greet my husband and the pair soon followed behind me. I was in Henry's arms when they came out and he looked at them with confusion.

"Surely not..." he began but then stopped.

"Yep. She's Aleric's mate."

"Damn. Father will not be happy about this."

"He'll have to get over it. Look what happened when he tried to keep Mal and Arista apart."

"I know, but will he?"

"It remains to be seen, dear. I'm heading to the glen. Bring me those chairs when you're ready?"

"I will, I just need to get a drink, then I'll be out."

I left him, and Aleric and Edana followed along, barely able to walk because they couldn't watch their feet and each other at the same time. It was adorable—the hard, stony woman I'd met earlier was now a woman who blushed and seemed somehow soft and sweet. Love did crazy things.

I spent the evening with my family, and Henry's family, as we placed chairs, an arbor, and ribbons in a variety of places. The flowers would be added by Henry's sister in the morning, and my mother and aunts were preparing the food. By the end of the night, Edana seemed to be lost in lust and more than a little bit confused. I couldn't say much to her though, not without revealing things I wasn't even sure I fully understood yet.

I watched her with Aleric and saw the way they danced around each other. They were going to burst into flames at any minute, and I just hoped she was prepared to have her life turned totally upside down. I hadn't been, but I'd managed to get through it. For all of her hard outer shell, I suspected Edana might be the weakest of us all. I would hate to see her hurt and hoped that she had a much easier time with it all than either Arista or I had experienced. Mine hadn't been so bad, actually, but Arista's had been a nightmare. If only I'd known then that fate wasn't done with any of us yet.

13

HENRY

"Ah, the old ball and chain." Mary sat down on a chair left for her by my brothers. We were all outside, sat around the fire pit I'd dug myself, watching the stars come out in the sky.

Willow and her bunch were inside doing their nails and slathering stuff on their skin. Apparently, Mary didn't want any part of that. She was welcome to stay outside with us, and avoid it all, but I suspected a part of her only refused because she didn't want to be seen as soft in any way around any of us. That, and I was her brother, so she would want to be with me, naturally.

"She isn't either of those things, Mary." I crushed her to me in a hug, and she gave me a thump on the arm for my efforts. I rubbed at the spot, Mary was no weakling, and grinned at her. "She's the green to my grass, the sun to my shine, the..."

"Oh, spare me, brother! I was only teasing! Please, don't make me unload that dinner on you!" We'd ordered pizzas for everybody, the first time either Mary or Aleric had tasted it and both had consumed two whole pizzas on their own, they were so infatuated with the taste and texture.

"Well, after what you ate, that's quite a lot, so I'll just keep my thoughts to myself then."

"You'll find a mate, one day, Mary. Then you'll see," Mal called to her from across the fire and I showed him a fist of unison.

"You tell her, brother."

"It looks like Aleric's in line next, not me," Mary quipped, her eyes cutting to Aleric. He'd gone quiet again, his eyes on the house where Edana was.

"I think you're right. Look at him. Totally oblivious to us."

Aleric was the youngest of us all, and the quietest of us all too.

With his golden looks, we'd all expected a child full of laughter and light, but we'd got a rather gloomy, brooding poet who hated being a soldier instead. He did his duties and took them seriously, but he'd rather write a sonnet than wield a sword. It didn't show in his physique or his abilities, so we let him have his fun.

"She's stunning, isn't she?" Aleric's voice broke over

the crackle of the flames and we all stared at him. "I've never seen anyone so beautiful."

"She's your mate, Aleric, but yes, she is beautiful." That came from Malcolm, the diplomatic one of the bunch.

"It's more than that though. She's special."

"We all think our mates are special, Aleric. You'll be alright, man." Mal patted our brother's shoulder and gave us all a knowing grin.

"We've all been there, well, except Mary," I pointed out. "We can't tease him, we know how it is."

"Ah, but isn't that why we tease him, Henry? We know how it turns your brains to mush."

"True, but it also brings clarity, and changes your outlook. I'm glad he's found his mate." I left my hopes for Mary unspoken.

"I hope it skips me altogether. I don't want to turn into the kind of saps you lot have." She shuddered and looked into the flames. "I'd rather keep my mind and my body as my own, thank you very much."

"You think that now. If it happens though, you'll know your life was empty before." I couldn't help the words, they were true. "I thought I had all I wanted until Willow came into my life. Now, there's nothing else I want but her."

"See? You've turned into a fool. Why, Mal was willing to give up the throne to keep his mate. Why would I want to be so dependent on someone else when I can make my own happiness?"

She couldn't understand, and wouldn't until she found her own mate, so I didn't argue.

"Do you think it's a curse?" Aleric's voice broke the silence again. "Do you think fate has decided that we are bad, and has decided to fuck us all over royally so we breed ourselves out of existence?"

"What?" Mary looked at him as if he'd grown another head, I think we all did.

"Think about it, why else would fate give us hunter mates? It makes no sense."

"Well, I'm a woman and only women are hunters, so I guess that blows that theory all to hell. I can pass along the dragon DNA as easily as you lot can." She laughed, but I noticed an air of tension around that laugh.

"I suppose fate could be exceedingly cruel to you and give you a female mate, Mary. You would never have children, but such pairings aren't uncommon."

"True, but I don't see it happening. This seems to be about breeding, making babies, so fate will ignore me. I can't have a female mate because we're meant to *mate*, aren't we? That seems to be the point of all of this."

"You're right." I let Mary off the hook and let it go. "Still, Aleric may be on to something. Why else would fate give us slayer mates? Galen is obviously a dragon, so that didn't work out, but any females might be both. Or neither. We never know, do we?"

"True. I guess we aren't meant to know and won't until fate decides it's time for us to know." Mary kicked another log onto the fire and we watched sparks fly from the pit. I'd lined it with rocks and fire bricks, so it was safe. With a water hose nearby, there was little chance of a fire spreading, even on the windy top of this hill.

I wondered about whether she actually wanted such a bleak life. Then I reminded myself Mary couldn't know what joy Willow brought to me or what joy Arista brought to Malcolm. And now Aleric would know that joy as well.

Tomorrow, I'd make her my bride. I wasn't sure how it would change anything between us, if it truly would, but I knew it was expected of us. I liked the idea either way, my mate and my wife. There was a double commitment in there somewhere. Fate had brought us together, choice would make us married. It was an example my world would understand, I hoped.

That brought my thoughts back to the wolves. They couldn't understand this either, but it would show what they were throwing away by breaking our laws. A chance at total happiness. Maybe it was our fate to slowly decline, anyway. Perhaps they were fighting nature, blighting us all with their demand for their continued existence at the expense of others. It was a stain on us all for sure.

"You're thinking grim thoughts," Willow whispered to me as she wrapped her arms around my neck from behind.

"You caught me while I was distracted, princess. How are you?" I kissed the side of her cheek and placed my hands over hers.

"I'm alright, my love. Do you want anything?" Her lips were right beside my ear when she spoke the words in a low voice, only for me to hear.

"You know I always want you, Willow." Heat singed each word and I felt her shiver in response.

"Well, you'll have to wait until tomorrow. We have a house full of guests." She brushed her hand through my hair, her breasts pressed into the back of my head.

Want filled me, and I looked at our guests. Would they notice if I dragged her off into the woods?

"Of course they'd notice, dear, but do you think they'd blame us?" There was a tremor to her words. She wasn't as unaffected as she'd like to pretend.

"I don't." I stood up and pulled her by the hand to the woods. I shifted and took her on my back at the same time. She was in a nightgown and robe, so it wouldn't take too long to get inside of her.

I flew her to a rather sturdy tree with thick limbs, landed, and had her against the tree with my cock buried inside of her before she could even get a good grip around my waist with her legs.

"You tempted me," I growled against her neck as I moved within her eager body. She was always ready for me.

I gripped her full breasts, my fingers teasing at her nipples until she came with a quiet cry of release. Something drove me, some deep need that I didn't understand. I knew she could take a little rough treatment and thrust into her with desperation. From the first touch of her hands on me to the moment I slid into her, want had filled me, and I needed what only Willow could give me. She cradled my head to her neck as I moved within her. My breath tore from my chest in desperate gasps, until at last, thank fuck, at last, the pressure eased, and I let go within her.

Maybe it was the talk of not needing a mate, a moment of fear that Willow would one day come to the same conclusion, but I knew I needed her. I needed her more than I'd ever needed her in that moment, and my lips found hers as a long cry of a satisfaction ripped from my throat.

"I am yours, you are mine. Nothing will change that, Henry." She continued to soothe me, her fingers on my cheek, then in my hair as waves of pleasure shook me to my core. She was all I needed. My woman.

She smiled at me as I came back to her, as my mind calmed, and my breath leveling. "Sorry."

I felt my cheeks heat and looked away as I let her body slide away from mine. The tree was huge, and the spot I'd chosen was actually two limbs that had fused together. We sat on the branches, our hands twined together as she leaned against me.

"I don't know what our future holds, Henry, I can't pretend to know, but I do know, it's *our* future. Not mine, not yours, but ours. It will be alright, whatever fate brings us next."

"Don't challenge fate, Willow. I've recently learned what a bitch it can be."

"You're right. But I know we were put together for a reason. I love you, and whether that's fate, chemicals, insanity, I don't care, I love you."

"I love you, Willow. Fuck mates, I love you, no matter what caused it. You caused it, actually. I couldn't love if you weren't you. I would want you, I'd want to be with you, but love? I don't think even fate can fake that."

"Perhaps not." She sighed, and I knew she was tired. Her pregnancy was progressing at a normal pace for her, but she was tired, and with the added burden of pregnancy, that meant she was actually exhausted.

"Let me get you to bed, princess. Come with me." I cradled her in my arms, shifted, and flew her to our home. I shifted before I left the edge of the woods and walked with her into the house.

"Sleep well, my bride. I'll see you in the morning." We'd planned an early wedding so we could escape to the honeymoon later.

"Good night, my love." She was asleep before I left the room. I went back out to the fire and found my brothers and sister still there.

Not a single one said a word about my sudden disappearance, and I retook my position by the fire. Tomorrow was a big day in more ways than one. Malcolm was the one who brought that touchy subject up.

"Do you think she'll be able to handle so many of us at once?" I knew what he meant. There'd be at least twenty dragons in that glen tomorrow, not just my family.

"I think she will." I hope she will. So far, she hadn't even felt a buzz with my siblings around. That was a good sign.

"We'll keep an eye on everything for you. Don't worry. At the least sign she's about to freak out we'll get the other dragons out of there."

"It's just her I'm worried about. There are more of her family at this wedding. And this new cousin too. She's been dormant for a long time, but who knows?"

"She hasn't reacted to us at all," Aleric pointed out without me having to name Edana. I grinned at him.

"Yeah, Willow didn't either, until I, uh, woke her up." I was about to say nailed her, but that was just crude as fuck, so I didn't. It still made me smirk though.

"We'll just have to wait and see, fellas," Mary said, her eyes on the flames again. It was going to be a long day for all of us. We risked exposure and death if anything went wrong, and it weighed on all of us. I had some of the security team coming in for more than one reason.

"I doubt any of us would be a match for a pack of hunters though, to be honest," Malcolm said, redirecting us.

"None of them realize how powerful they are," Mary replied.

"That's probably a good thing. It will keep all of us safe, in the long run, if they don't remember most of their powers." Malcolm again.

"Is it right though?" Aleric didn't look happy.

"No, but we need to make peace with them, brother. We aren't the same as our ancestors, they aren't the same as theirs. We all have heinous acts in our past, done by our ancestors. We have to move past that. Especially as all of our numbers have dwindled throughout the worlds, not just ours."

"It's not dropped much in some of them," Malcolm reminded me.

"You're right, but we know those worlds are either dragon free or slayer free now. There's no conflict there now. There's no reason to be worried about populations in those places."

"Unless their numbers start to drop too," Mary said. "It really does look like there's more going on here than we thought. This isn't just our world that's gone mad."

"Tonight isn't the time to discuss it. There's time to do this later. Tonight, we toast Henry. Congratulations and all the joys of the future to you, brother." Malcolm raised his glass to me and my siblings joined in. He'd brought a barrel of dragon wine and we were determined to finish it before the sun came up. Tomorrow was going to be a good day, no matter what I had to do to make sure of it.

14

WILLOW

I stared out at the dawn as the sun began its climb into the sky. Birds filled the air with their morning song, a dog barked in the distance, and a soft breeze made the leaves in the trees dance. It was going to be a beautiful day.

"Nothing can match how beautiful you are, honey." My mom came up behind me and hugged me around the waist. I put my hands over hers and stared down at her face. I was taller than her by a good six inches. I'd had to look down at her since I was about 14.

"I'll love you forever, Momma, you know that, don't you?"

"Of course I do, Willow. I'll love you all the days of my life too, darlin', don't ever doubt that. What do you want for breakfast?"

"I'm not sure I can eat." I felt her hand tense on my

belly, and she gave me a look.

"You need toast, sweetheart. And a hot chocolate. I'll make you some then we'll turn you into a bride." She trotted off to the kitchen happily and I watched her go.

Edana came down next, and she looked at me in front of the screen door. "I always knew you'd be a beautiful bride. From the first time you put on that dress I made out of a pillowcase, I knew you'd be just perfect."

She brushed a lock of hair out of my face, her grey eyes smiling. "I can't believe I'm here with you."

"It's odd, isn't it? I haven't seen you in over 13 years, but it feels like it was only yesterday." I took her hand in mine, sensing some odd connection that joined us.

"It does. I'm glad your mom found me. I'm so happy you asked for me."

"That wouldn't have more to do with Aleric than me, would it?" I grinned when her cheeks turned pink.

"No, it does but it doesn't. I think it was time for me to come home." She patted my cheek and then made her own way to the kitchen.

The rest of the morning was taken up with hair straighteners, a dusting of makeup I never wore, hairspray, makeup setting spray, and a flurry as silk and tulle settled over my head. The top of my dress was fitted lace, the bottom a poof of tulle that mimicked a cloud. I'd chosen it because it reminded me of how Henry made me feel. The heart in the neckline just set it all off.

Lace sleeves covered my arms, and we'd arranged my hair in a knot on the top of my head. I was made up, hair done, and dressed in a way that was not familiar. I looked beautiful, or so the faces around me said. Mom's eyes were even filled with tears.

"I waited for this day. I knew it would have to come, but I never imagined you'd look so... perfect, Willow. So absolutely perfect."

I crushed her in a hug, and then we walked down and out of the house together. She walked me up the aisle as the song played. It could have been a Slipknot song for all I knew, all I felt was her hand in mine, the way my heart pounded, and the pure love that washed over me when I saw Henry's eyes on me. That was the goal, reach him before tears broke from my own eyes.

The official spoke, words were said, I repeated some more, and then his ring was on my finger, mine was on his, and our lips were together as the crowd around us cheered. It was all far too surreal to even know if it had been perfect or not. I watched him, his eyes when he smiled, his lips when he spoke, and gave him my hand when I was told to.

My husband, this dragon, this man, was now my husband. The tears came and I broke tradition and threw my arms around his neck. I had a complete family now. Our family. He'd given me more than just himself, he'd given me a family of my own.

We walked back down the aisle to a shower of rose petals thrown by our guests who sang out cheers and laughed as we ran down to the area where we planned to hold the reception. My brain turned back on when he pulled me to him for one more kiss. Our guests filtered into the reception area, but we didn't care, we only knew each other. We pulled apart and I had a smile on that would not stop, even when it began to hurt to smile.

I was too happy not to smile. I hadn't wanted this life, but it was mine, and I'd kill anyone that tried to take it from me now. I smiled at dragons, I shook their hands, I hugged his brothers and sister, I took the kiss his father placed on my cheek and smiled at him without a single twitch. I made it through the day, and most importantly, I didn't kill anyone by accident.

I looked out at a sea of smiling, happy faces, and breathed a sigh of relief. I hadn't realized how worried I'd been. Not that something would ruin the big day, but that I myself would ruin the day with uncontrollable rage at my guests. I'd made it through the day, and everyone was still breathing. That was the best gift we'd had.

I noted faces, and names, but didn't really notice any of them until a group of brothers came up with some of the most beautiful women I'd ever seen at their sides. They were late arrivals and Henry and I were on our way out when they all showed up.

"Willow, these are my cousins, Kane, Cade, Jadrian, and Jacob Alexander. And these are their wives, Damesha, Jacqui, Sabrina, and Allana." Henry introduced me to his rather gorgeous extended family members, and I stared at them in awe.

All were temptingly beautiful in their own ways, and they all seemed to have some kind of magical quality to them. They were women I'd like to get to know, and men to be admired.

"It's very nice to meet all of you."

"They live in your world, but the brothers are very special shifters, they're shapeshifters. They can be anything they choose."

"Oh now, that's convenient."

"It can come in handy," the one named Kane said with a lilt of laughter. He had a boyish grin and mischievous eyes. His wife, Damesha, put her arm around his waist and grinned at me.

"Especially if you like water." That seemed to sober the one named Jadrian for some reason and I knew I'd have to get the story behind that at some point. Right now, I had a honeymoon to get to.

"I'm sorry to leave, but we have an appointment to keep," Henry said with an apologetic tone. He gave me a wink, as they all adopted knowing smiles. I grinned at them unabashedly.

"Yeah, an appointment." I wiggled my eyebrows and

they all laughed. I felt at ease around them all, though we'd only just met. I gave a light wave of my hand as we left the gorgeous family. I would have to invite them all to dinner sometime, I decided as we walked away.

"Are you ready to visit the land under the sea, my princess?" Henry smiled down at me as we walked to the car, our adoring family calling out words of love and goodbye to us.

"Wait." I stopped for a minute, my arm on the door of the driver's side. Henry had no license and didn't know how to drive. "I'm really a princess now, aren't I?"

"Of course, you are, my love. You are Princess Willow of Henry, or Princess Willow, Countess of Wirkster now. Whichever you prefer."

"Willow seems good enough to me." I shoved yards of tulle into the car and we laughed when I tried to buckle my seatbelt and the tulle just kept puffing up. He held it down for me, and I stuffed most of it under me so that I could drive away, a wave of the hand a final goodbye.

"I guess I should have changed dresses."

"It's our first challenge and we conquered it together, so hard." He tried out another saying from my world and it made me laugh.

"So hard!" I repeated in a dark voice, and we laughed again.

Nothing could spoil life now.

15

WILLOW

"Your brother wants you," I said from the heavenly bed in our suite beneath the sea.

I looked out of the window on my side of the bed and saw a shark swim lazily behind a family of seahorses. I was still amazed that we were actually in the ocean in a hotel full of people who lived beneath the sea.

"What does he want?" Henry's arm was thrown over his head, he was exhausted. He'd earned every moment of that exhaustion, I thought, as I waited for Malcolm to buzz around in my head again.

"It seems there's something going on with your father."

"What? What's wrong now?" We couldn't get a cell-phone signal under the water, even if Henry had one, and I had to relay the images Mal sent me to Henry.

I saw Godwin heading into the forest behind our

house, and knew Malcolm was following him. "He says your father has been acting strange since we left. He's been watching him and saw him head off into the woods and is now following him."

"What is that old man up to now?" I gave Henry a look. His father might be old, but he didn't necessarily look old. He was still fit and healthy looking. Dragons didn't age as humans did, after all. Especially in their own world.

"Mal says there are wolves there, he can smell them." Sure enough, as Mal stepped further into the woods, a group of five wolves appeared, in their human forms.

"That's Zlo, a Russian wolf from your world. What's he doing at our house?"

We watched through Mal's eyes as Godwin, normally a very regal man, approached the wolves with something akin to deference. Zlo handed Godwin something, and Godwin fell to his knees with his hand above his mouth.

"Is he pouring something into his mouth?" I knew in that moment that our honeymoon was over before it had even begun.

Cade Alexander is here with me. I'm sorry Willow, but if what he says is true, I need Henry here. You two have to come back.

I sighed with disappointment but knew there was little that could be done.

Did Cade really say it was vampire blood? I asked.

Yes, it seems to be a problem from the wolves of your world. Just get home and we'll talk about it in person. Sorry, Willow.

I sighed again and looked over at Henry.

"Time to head back to the real world." He'd seen it all from me and let out his own sigh. "Why the fuck would my father drink vampire blood? That's just stupid."

"Mal said he'd explain when we get home." I got out of the bed, opened the case we'd brought, and put on a pair of jeans and a dark blue long-sleeved shirt with a hood. It could get cold on Henry's back.

It didn't take long to get back to the house, and it was a good thing we went back. Chaos seemed to reign as people walked in and out of rooms, and plans were being made. Our home now looked like a war room with maps tacked on the wall with putty, and the Alexander clan and Henry's clan directing soldiers to different areas of the house.

"What the hell?" I asked as I looked around. "What have you done to my house?"

Henry placed a soothing hand on the small of my back and walked me into the kitchen. We found Cane there with Malcolm at the pine table we'd bought to feed an entire army. It was covered in papers, pictures, and more maps now.

"Hi, Willow, Henry! Sorry to take over your home,

but we seem to have a major problem that we were unaware of. We thought it best to stay in your world since this seems to be the point of origin." Mal stood up and ushered us to our own table.

I glared at him, but he just gave me a smile that melted my chagrin away. They all seemed to be able to do that to me now. I huffed anyway and sat down.

"What's going on then?" Henry asked as he took his own seat beside me.

"It seems the wolves in this world had other plans to cause disruption. The Alexanders here wiped most of them out with the help of their own clans spread around their world. They were selling vampire blood to shifters, apparently it's an intoxicant that's a hundred times more addictive than cocaine is to humans."

"Yes, my brother, Jadrian, had a problem with it for a while." I turned to Cade when he took over speaking. "It causes a euphoric feeling and can make even humans feel like they can keep up with the physiology of shifters. Jadrian was using it to try to fulfill the duties we didn't realize were too much for a mortal person to handle. His wife, Allana, made him a shifter, and that took care of the problem, but it can be very addictive to shifters of any kind. If they've infiltrated your world, then we need to stop it, now."

Sabrina came in and took a place at the table. She was a vampire, I realized as I watched her. A very beautiful one. "My people aren't all moral people. Some are quite evil, as your mythology says. They'd sell their own creator if it bought them what they wanted. The remaining wolves have used them to sell their blood to other humans and shifters in our world. If the king of the dragon world is using it, we have a problem."

Something about her drew me, but I don't think she did it on purpose. She was just... seductive. I looked away, rather confused about the whole thing. Henry had told me vampires were real before I met the clan, but she was just something I hadn't expected. She smiled at me, a smile that was an apology at the same time as it was reassurance that she understood.

"So what do we do?" Henry asked finally, his gaze on his brothers. Apparently, he didn't feel the slightest bit of allure from the beautiful vampire.

"We prepare for battle. This is an opening shot, and they've already scored a victory, I'm afraid," Cane said, and Malcolm nodded in agreement.

"Wait, we only just got married. Can't we put this whole battle mode thing off for even a few days?"

"It can't wait, Willow. We have to start to dig out the cells and put a stop to this before it goes any further."

I looked at Henry and knew he was right. Damn it all!

16

HENRY

We were about to take a big chance, a huge chance, and Willow shook nervously on my back as I descended to the landing pad. I was needed in my world, and it was time we took that chance. Willow had changed, she'd learned far more control outside of the Amazun world than she had in it, and the wedding had gone off without a hitch. It was time to test her in my world.

"How do you feel?" I asked as I shifted and set her down on the ground. I examined her face and body for signs of stress, but there were none.

"Good. Okay." I could tell by her shortness that she was tense, but she didn't seem to be twitchy. That was good.

"Let's go inside." The current plan was to hunt down the factions in our own world and trace Zlo's dealings here. Then we could find out more about how this all tied to my father.

"It's not so bad." Willow broke into my thoughts as we walked through the halls of my father's castle. "Much better than last time."

She looked around with curiosity this time, not fear. She didn't feel threatened now, she wasn't so afraid, and she had far more confidence in herself. This would be alright.

I took her to the hall where the meeting between the wolves, bears, and my father would take place. It was a meeting to discuss the plans to address the lack of mates and children amongst the wolves and the bears.

Unlike the Alexander clan, who could shift into any animal they wanted to, we only had shifters who could change into one animal and one alone. You didn't get to choose which, you just were.

We arrived just as my father made another refusal to the pleas of the bears.

"You cannot kidnap human women from other worlds. It is simply against the law here."

Willow went still beside me. She stared around the room and her gaze settled on my father. She was okay, so I followed her gaze. He seemed far twitchier than she did, as if he was nervous, or had bugs crawling on his skin. His behavior had been rather erratic of late. He had tried to kill Arista and Malcolm not so long ago, after all, and now he sat there scratching at his beard, at his head, his arms, and kept moving around as if he couldn't sit still.

Why hadn't I noticed any of this before?

He'd looked healthy lately, really healthy, and had seemed to be more harsh than usual, but he hadn't looked like this. He sat on his throne, his scarlet and gold robes unclean and in disarray. Something was very wrong here.

"Sire, we know the laws. We're dying out though, and we have no other solution." This from a bear named Bjorn.

"We're dying off, and you don't seem to care, my king." A woman named Lupe, of the wolf delegation, came forward.

"What would you have me do, Lupe?" My father sighed and opened his hands. "There will be no kidnapped human women in this world. I can't say it enough times."

"What if they are willing to come?" Bjorn asked, his voice hopeful.

"I'm afraid that won't be acceptable either." Father sat up straight then, as if he had been hit by lightning. "Oh."

I felt Willow move around beside me, her gaze on my father. She seemed engrossed in what he was doing, and to be honest, his odd behavior had my attention too.

"Well, perhaps..." Godwin looked confused, as though

he was surprised at what he'd said. "Perhaps if they are willing..." He slapped his hand over his mouth, his eyes wide. What was wrong with him?

The whole room started to buzz as my father seemed to struggle with his own body. "Perhaps if they are willing, we can allow some exceptions to the laws."

The entire room gasped. Godwin had just wavered on a *law*! It was more than the wolves or the bears could have ever hoped for.

It was, in fact, more than I could believe. I watched my father twitch again, his hand jerked away from his mouth and his eyes went wide.

"This is my decree..." He paused, and it looked as if he was fighting for control of his own tongue. What was wrong with him? Why didn't anybody check on him?

"Wolves and bears may take human women as mates, if the woman signs a contract that says she will never ask to go back to her world, that swears she will never attempt to go back to her own world, and that she is fully aware of her companion's state of being a shifter. All children born of these unions will be citizens of this world and will not be allowed to go to the world of their mother's. If the mate is a man, for a female shifter, then the same must be agreed and signed. Other than under these circumstances, you will not be allowed to kidnap mates from the other worlds, at all. I will not have it. Am

I clear?" His voice slurred at the end, but it was clear to all what he meant.

It was a solid decision, though it did put us in danger of being discovered and revealed to Willow's world. In truth, I think it was the only decision that could be made if my father wanted to maintain peace in our land. Something was wrong with him, but it was good to see a little bit of his fairness return.

We hadn't forgotten what we saw in the woods, or rather what Malcolm saw, but we did have to maintain a balance for now. We were investigating and making an attempt to maintain some semblance of normality in our world. For a moment, I felt overwhelmed, the way Willow must have felt in the beginning of our relationship. So many worlds, so much at stake, so little time to absorb it all.

Six months ago, I was a soldier, a man with his own life, and a prince. Now, I was a husband, a mate, and soon to be a father. I lived a double-life, and the constant flights between my world and hers, the constant turmoil from the problems in both of our worlds, made my head spin. I walked out of the hall and Willow followed.

"Are you alright, Henry?" she asked, her hand on my back to comfort me.

"Yeah, I just need some sleep. I'm a little drained.

Watching father was a little hard too. What's wrong with him?"

She had an odd expression on her face, but then it smoothed out. Gas, maybe?

I led her back to my own home, and she went down to the kitchen to retrieve some wine. She came back up to my bedroom—our bedroom now—and slid into bed with me, two glasses in hand. One held apple juice and the other wine. It was a dark red wine, dragon wine, and full of flavor. I took a sip, and let my head fall to my pillows. With her beside me, the duvet over me to keep me warm, and my world still slightly spinning, I let my eyes close.

"I just want an hour of sleep. That's all." I fell asleep before I'd even finished my glass of wine.

I fell into dreams of Willow, our future together, and the many ways we could explore our passion for each other. In my dreams, she was the same wildly passionate lover I had in real life. She danced through the jungle, away from me, only to turn back with a laugh or a smile as I chased her. Sunlight danced on her silky skin, in her hair, and I knew she was the most beautiful woman I'd ever seen.

Everything about her caught my gaze. To someone else her eyes might be too far apart, her shoulders a little too muscular, or her waist not narrow enough, but to me, she was perfect. Her waist was the perfect size to span my large hands around, her shoulders were muscular because she played the piano, she played the music that soothed the dragon inside of me. Her eyes revealed the things she thought, the love she had for me, the things that amused her.

I caught her in the jungle foliage and fell with her onto a bed of flowers. Their delicate petals brushed our skin, tiny fingers that delighted the senses. Her legs wrapped around my waist, her tongue wrapped around mine, and the world was perfect again. I closed my eyes, and when I opened them, I had her in my arms, and we were in a world of darkness, the yellowish-green glow of fungi the only light. Her eyes glowed within the darkness, a golden-brown honey that soothed my mind.

A blink found us in our home in her world, our bed, her old bed, cradled us as we danced together, our bodies joined where she straddled me. I watched her as she teased herself, her fingers tight on her own nipples. I loved it when she made herself moan like that. She'd done that a few times for me now, teasing herself into an orgasm as I watched.

I loved to watch her, every aspect of her fascinated me. The dream morphed again, and we were in one of the establishments in another world. A house where sex was bought and sold, where people who couldn't be themselves acted out whatever desire they had together, for payment or for free. It was a house where anything went; a place my father had taken me a long time ago. I walked down a long hallway, searching for something, not sure what until I saw Willow in a red corset, red panties, with long red leather boots strapped over her legs. The leather came up to her thighs.

She sat with her arms behind her to prop her up with her breasts thrust out. Her legs were open, bent at the knees. Her hair was in a long braid down her back, and her eyes were dark with kohl. She was sensuality, temptation, and deliverance in one promising package. I walked into the room and she pulled her thighs together.

"What can I do for you, sir?" Her smirk told me she knew exactly what she could do.

I walked up to her, my dick already hard and ready for those ruby red lips she'd painted with gloss. I wanted to see them wrapped around my dick.

"What do you offer?"

"Oh, I'm only here for you, sir. I am yours alone." She moved then, a slow crawl across the bed, her eyes held mine captive. She was like a snake as she moved across that huge bed of black lace and satin.

"Open for me." Her eyes held mine still, but her red-tipped nails stroked down the fasteners of my pants. I popped the buttons free and let her open the panels to free my aching flesh. She gasped, that same gasp she'd made the first time she saw me naked. It often replayed in my mind.

Her fingers danced over my pants and they disappeared, while her other hand gripped me, strong and eager. Her hand stroked me just the way I'd taught her to. My own reached out to stroke under her chin.

"Are you going to suck my dick for me, princess?"

Her eyes blazed up to mine. "No, but I am going to fuck it, sir."

I shivered, her response a naughty defiance that I found tantalizing.

A wet heat enveloped me, and that's when the dream broke. The liquid walls that gripped me brought me back to reality. Willow was naked, straddled over me, and I was deep inside of her.

"You'll have to tell me about that dream you were having later, Henry," she purred above me, but she was too lost in how it felt to have me inside of her to say anything more. I heard how wet she was when her slick flesh ground against me, and her clit pressed into me. She was going to get herself off without any help from me at all if I didn't do anything.

I took her breasts in my hands, my thumbs directly over her nipples to stroke them into tight peaks. "You're so wet, Willow. What were you thinking about when you decided to ride my dick, princess?"

"I was thinking about dark rooms, the sounds of

others as they found their pleasure, and watching other people."

"Were you indeed?" This was a new side to her. One I hadn't known existed, but I liked it. "You want to listen to other people fuck? Watch them?" I gave her an extra thrust as her walls swallowed around me when I spoke. "Do you want to see their pleasure, Willow? To hear it as I fuck into you?"

"I do, Henry. Fuck, I do want it. I want it so much." Her fingers fluttered on my chest, and one went down between her thighs to work the throbbing pulse of her clit. She was so close her soul was already weaving into mine.

I wasn't far behind her. Another gasping sigh or an accidental touch as she moved on me, seeking her own pleasure, would send me over the edge. It was... just... right... there...

"Willllllllooooow..."

Her name sighed out of me as she pulsed around me and I pulsed into her. The world became the blue and white smoke of our souls that threaded together into a light blue singularity. I poured myself into her as I became her, and she swallowed every single drop of me as she became me.

"I can't stop loving you, Henry. Fuck, I can't stop. I don't even want to try, but I couldn't if I did. It's so good, baby. Loving you is just so perfect."

Her words intruded on my mind, and I had no idea how she found the ability to speak. All I could do was groan wildly as she sucked every inch of me with her tight pussy. It didn't matter, she was right, I couldn't stop loving her either. There was just no way it could ever happen. There was nothing more perfect than this.

17

WILLOW

"What do you mean, you influenced my father's choice?" I heard his voice rumble in his chest beneath my ear. Shit, I'd let my thoughts slip.

I sat up and rolled off him.

"He was about to make a mistake, Henry. The best solution was to let the bears and wolves bring in their mates, if they had them. Your father's stubbornness was about to create a war!"

"That's his decision to make, not yours!" Fury poured from him in waves and I watched, shocked, as he stood up and put his clothes back on.

"Where are you going?"

"To ask him if he made that choice or if you really have developed the power to influence people's decisions. Maybe you only think you did it." He spat the words out and hurt flooded my chest.

"Henry..."

"No, Willow. This might be worse than blasting the fuck out of the courtyard the first time I brought you here. What happens when he makes another decision you don't like? Will you force him to change his mind again?" He paused and deflated for a moment. "I know you thought you were doing what was best, but you are not the king. You can't... fuck... I'll be back in a little while."

He brushed his hands through his hair as he left, the anger back again. I pulled the covers around me and tried to blink away my tears. It was a new symptom of my pregnancy this week. I cried at the drop of a hat. I'd put it off at the wedding, but now I was in a flood of tears again. It had to be the pregnancy, I wasn't normally this weepy.

I'd only done what I thought was best and now Henry was saying it might have been worse than my light. I suppose it was. I'd imposed my own will on a king. I ducked my head down to my knees and bit the skin there to ease the pain inside of me. Okay, maybe it had been a stupid thing to do, but I could sense that the king wasn't in his right mind and the bears and wolves were on the edge of a revolt. If a little nudge in the right direction could avert that, why shouldn't I?

Henry was gone for a very long time and I used his bathtub to clean away the ache of the day. I found my stomach was larger than it had been the night before. The pregnancy had started to advance quickly here in this world. I wouldn't be able to stay here long at this rate. It would be hard to explain a pregnancy that lasted only a few months to others in my world. Of course, time passed quickly in my world, so maybe it would equal out?

It was too confusing, and I decided to wander through the house instead. I found a new addition from my last visit. A piano from my world sat in a corner of one room. I went to it and stroked the keys. Tuned perfectly.

I sat down and trilled out a melody that soon turned into an entire piece. I lost myself in the music the way I used to do. I poured the last few months of craziness into the music, and let out my current resentment towards Henry and his family. The piece turned into something totally new as I played fast and hard, my fingers pounding on the keys hard enough to make the notes reverberate around the room.

Clarity came as I played. Why the hell was Henry going to his father to tell him what I'd done? He knew the man already didn't trust either Arista or me, this would only make it worse. What did he think he'd accomplish by giving his dad a reason not to? I blushed because, for a change, Godwin would be right not to trust me. I'd made him say those words, I'd made him voice the new plan. He had fought me, but he'd done it anyway.

It might not have been the smartest choice to make, to take the will of a king away and replace it with my own, but if everyone but the king saw the sense in it, why shouldn't I do what was best for everybody? Fuck them all. Playing with their own lives to please one man was just stupid. I was angry now, and I went to the room to look through my clothes. I think it might just be time to head back to my own world, get some advice from my own people.

I dressed, just as tense now as I was before I'd taken a bath and played the piano. I needed the voices of my mother and my aunt to soothe me. I mentally reached out, but all were busy, Arista with baby Galen, my mom and aunt with some charity work, even Edana, wide-eyed and beautiful Edana who'd witnessed everything in my home that night before without a single question, had left and gone back to her own little world.

I couldn't talk to Mary, either. She was Henry's sister and the king's daughter. She was liable to come in and try to chop my head off with that massive sword I'd seen her wear as to tell me I'd done the right thing by infiltrating her father's brain. For the first time since Henry and I had first mated I felt... *alone*.

The word hurt, but it was right. We'd faced problems, we'd faced things that made us angry, that hurt us, that caused us anxiety, but those things had never been about actions we had taken that upset the other. This was our first real fight, I realized. I didn't like it at all.

Okay, maybe it wasn't exactly the right thing to do, but I didn't think it was wrong either. I'd saved them all a lot of grief by doing what I'd done. Surely they would see the sense in that? Laws could be changed, if Godwin had any sense he'd have done that at the first sign of trouble instead of obstinately sticking to old ways and old laws. He'd been on the verge of plunging his world into a civil war, and for what? The sake of tradition? It made no sense. Change the laws, adapt with the times, but never go back in time. That was just repeating a fool's mistake.

I thought about all I'd heard over the last couple of days. Godwin might be using vampire blood which created a feeling of euphoria and invincibility. Perhaps that was clouding his judgment. He'd been twitchy before I got into his brain, was he already needing another dose? Was it that addictive?

Maybe the vampires were the ones pulling the string and not Godwin, the wolves, or the bears. Maybe this was all some underhanded vampire trick? I'd liked Sabrina, the little I got to know of her, but she was a seductress, even when she wasn't trying to seduce her prey. I bit my lip and frowned over that thought. Prey? Ew!

Hadn't she turned Jacob, the youngest Alexander, into a vampire? I'd thought I'd heard a vague mention of Jacob being a vampire now. He had looked paler than the other brothers. Was she part of the plot too? I didn't know a lot about vampires, they were mythical creatures to me until I'd met Henry. Was she as committed to her mate and to the Alexander's as they thought?

I tapped my nails against the piano keys. None of it made any sense to me. I wasn't a stupid woman, but without all of the facts, I couldn't tease apart the puzzle, either. I waited, I had no way back to my world without a dragon to take me, and I started to fume. I was stranded here, at least until one of them came to take me home. If they took me home.

His father wouldn't try to imprison me, would he? My blood ran cold, and a shiver ran up my spine. He'd put Malcolm and Arista in a prison, he could do the same thing to me, couldn't he?

A knock came at the door before I could creep further into conspiracy theory land. Mary came in and looked around. She smiled when she saw me. She didn't know then.

"Hey, Willow. Where's Henry?" Mary looked around, didn't see her brother and came to sit by me on the couch.

"With your father. Listen, Mary, something's come up, could you run me back to my world?"

"You're not feeling... I don't know... twitchy are you?" She looked me over with concern and kind of leaned back away from me.

"No, nothing like that, I just need to get home." I didn't want to explain why, I didn't want to cry. All I wanted was to get back to my own bed where I could sob in peace.

It felt as if my eyeballs were about to bulge out of my head as I sat there and looked at her. I tried so hard not to cry, but it was about to be a battle I lost.

"Sure, honey. Do you need a bag or anything?"

My answer was to run up the stairs and grab the bag I hadn't even unpacked yet. I ran back down, and we took off from the house. I think she could sense the urgent need I had to get home and wanted to ask more about what was wrong but wisely held her tongue. She dropped me off and stayed long enough to have a mug of tea before she left again. The house was empty now, nobody had stayed once we returned from the honeymoon, and I felt as if a part of me was missing.

Henry wasn't there, of course it felt like that! Maybe the stupid thing wasn't the fact that I changed Godwin's mind, maybe the stupid thing was that I'd run away to hide. The thought of being imprisoned in his dungeon didn't appeal at all, and I'd taken the opportunity given to me and run like a rabbit that had spotted a hunter. No, it wasn't stupid to run at all.

The question was what would Henry do about it? What would his father do about it all? I wanted to hide, and for a moment, even considered how I might make my way back to the Amazuns. They wouldn't allow anyone to take me.

Calm down, Willow. Henry won't allow anything to happen to you. Besides, I'm still in your body. They won't do anything until my arrival anyway.

I perked up at my baby's words. *You're right. They'll wait to do anything until then. I'll have time to plead my case.*

It's really not that bad. If Godwin had made a sensible choice in the beginning...

Why didn't you say anything to me before I left, Marya? I felt so alone...

I was in my quiet time, Willow. I grew these things that dangle off the bottom of my legs during that time. Feet, I think you call them.

I laughed at the baby's description of her feet and then another thought occurred to me.

I can't have you in a hospital, can I?

No, you'll have to have a magical midwife of some kind. The fairies have good ones.

I was impressed with how well she knew the world she hadn't even been born into yet.

We are all old souls, recycled into new lives, Willow. When

I'm born, my slate will be wiped clean and I'll start all over again. Until then, I'll remain a shell of the person I used to be.

Do you know who you were? I was kind of surprised at Marya's revelations and the knowledge that she used to be someone else. Did she feel trapped right now?

No, I don't feel trapped, just eager to have another chance at life. I don't remember who I was before, I just have knowledge of the magical world, so I must come from there.

Sounds like you must. It would be interesting to know who you were, just to see how your lives change.

Ah, but that would take away the point of getting to have another chance, wouldn't it? If I knew who I was, if I was born fully cognizant of my past, I'd just wait to either make the same mistakes or try not to make them, and perhaps that in itself would be a mistake, mightn't it?

Damn, my baby is a philosopher! Wow!

I see your point, I thought. *So it's like the Hindu idea of reincarnation?*

They do have the better understanding of it all, yes. The only true Nirvana, though, is when we find our mates. That moment when your souls fuse together and you reach bliss, that's the only real Nirvana we'll ever know.

You must have been a shifter to know that. I felt a pang of sadness for my baby, to know about that, their former self must have experienced it. Would she be a shifter in this life?

I don't know what I'll be, Willow. I know I'm growing a

human body, but could there be a dragon soul within me? I don't know.

Will that make life hard for you? I remembered the words of the Amazun leader and worried.

It may, but I'll have your strength and Henry's to help me through it.

I hope you will. I hope we can guide you through life and make it easier for you.

It will be an odd life. We'll manage. You know, Henry does love you. He's loyal to his kind, and his king, but he loves you. It's not just the mating that fuses you, it's your love for each other.

You're right. I know you are. I panicked and ran. I should have waited for him.

Oh no, Godwin may have imprisoned you if you'd stayed, but you took that chance from him.

That's good then. I still thought it might have been a bad idea to run.

Sometimes the best path is the path of least resistance, Willow. You found it easier to leave the path that could be made harder if you'd stayed. It was a wise choice.

I can hope.

I need to sleep again, mother. I think I might be growing fingers now. There are nubs on my hands.

Oh my God, that's so cute! I wish I could see you!

Meh, I just look like an alien right now. Wait until I'm born, then you'll recognize me.

Go to sleep, little one, I think I'll join you.

I changed into a nightgown, crawled under the covers, closed the shutters with the remote control, and blocked the world out. I needed to rest, to stop my thoughts, if just for a little. Maybe Henry would be here when I woke up. I didn't know how I'd feel if he wasn't, but I'd deal with that when we got to it.

18

———

HENRY

"*B*anished?" I stared at my father, the words ringing in my ears.

"Yes, if your bride can't control herself, if she wants to make decisions for me, then she's banished from this world, Henry. End of the discussion." My father turned away from me and wrote something on a piece of paper at his desk in his bedchamber.

"Banished?"

"Yes, and if you choose to join, you'll be banished right along with her. I'll never be able to trust that the advice you give me, or the intelligence that you relay to me is not from her. Her actions have thrown everything into question, haven't they?" He looked up at me, his brow raised over his right eye.

Banished. Fuck.

"You know we can't be separated, Father. We'll both die."

"Of course you will. It's your choice, die for your king, or be with your mate. I should warn you though, I will have you stripped of your dragon. You will have to live—" he paused to shudder, "—as a human."

Somebody came in but I couldn't tear my eyes away from my father to see who it was. "You'll strip me of my dragon?"

"Yes, in a few hours the magicians will have erased her memory of this world, and of the dragons, and if you follow her, you'll be stripped of your dragon, though not of your memories." There was an evil gleam in my father's eyes as he said that last part, as if the thought of me being tortured by memories pleased him. It was almost as if he wasn't my father at all. "You have three hours to get her out of our world, if she's still here, or both her and the child will be destroyed by fire."

"What the fuck?" I kicked up out of my chair. The wood shattered into pieces as it flew out behind me hard enough to break against the wall. "You'll have her and my daughter burned? You're mad!"

"No, I'm fed up with you children and your hunters. Get out now, make your choice." He waved me away from his desk, and I stared at him, anger on my face, hatred in my heart.

"Come on, Henry, let me help you." It was Mary, and

she led me from the room. Her own face was confused, hurt, and angry. "Willow isn't here. She's at your home in her world."

"How?" I tried to slow my raging heart, but it wouldn't listen. I was angry beyond words, and even the knowledge that Willow was safe in her world didn't help. How dare he? How dare he threaten to destroy the life of my child? Of my mate? I could take my punishment, it would be hard, but I could take it. A death threat against my family though? That was more than even a son could stand.

"I took her there. What the fuck happened?" Mary stared up at me, her question on her face.

"Willow influenced Father to change his mind about the human women. I told him, like an asshole. I should have known better. That man isn't our father, I don't know who he is, but that's not the man that raised us."

"I think it's the vampire blood. It can change who you are from what I've learned about it so far." Mary had been researching the substance and its effects on humans and magicals. "It really is as addictive as the Alexanders said it was, and one tough drug to match."

"That's just great. A junkie for a ruler. Great." I stalked away from the castle and to the flight pad. There was nothing I wanted to take with me and planned to leave immediately.

"Henry, wait. Stop. Don't just leave. Think about

what you might need if Father really does strip your dragon away. I don't think he can, but if he's found a way, then think. What will you need for your life with Willow and that baby?"

"I'll need money in her world, more than anything else." I changed directions and stalked to the house. I picked up a bag and started to fill it with jewelry and other valuables I might be able to sell. I had a rather large fortune in diamonds alone. They were dragon-made, but her world would not be able to tell the difference. I took the books about our history and added them to the bag. My child deserved to know where she came from. I also picked up a few weapons. If Father really did make me a mortal, I wanted to know I could defend my family.

I packed some of my clothes, things that I knew Willow liked.

"I'll contact the fixer we have there, the one that is working on the papers you need there. I'll light a fire under them to get those papers done."

"What if this is the last time I see you, Mary? Or home?" The consequences of leaving weren't lost on me.

"Then you'll have made the right choice for you and your family, Henry. Go. I'll try to come to you when I can."

She turned me around and pushed me out of the door of my own home. I didn't have time to waste, but I also couldn't believe any of this had really happened. I flew to Willow, to her world, to a new life maybe. I hung in the air for a while, to feel the wind on my face as it screamed over my wings. I stretched my muscles as I climbed, then fell, only to climb again. If this is the last time I might fly, I wanted it to be memorable.

I'd give it all up, and gladly, for Willow, but I needed this one last moment of flight. Just in case. Wind tore at my armored leather skin, but it didn't win, it never would against a dragon's flesh. I blew a flame across the sky, perhaps the last flame I'd ever breathe out, and finally came to rest on a tree outside of our bedroom window. Willow had the shutters closed, but I knew she was there. I could feel her.

Would that change? I wondered. If Father actually managed to strip my dragon away, would I still be mated to her? Would I be magical at all? I felt the branch beneath my much smaller claws, and took one final breath before I let go, and shifted as I landed. It was a hard thing to give up, this being a dragon business, but if it meant I stayed with my mate and my child, then so be it. I could live without it. It wouldn't be easy, I'd have to learn to drive, to let others fly me in planes, to do things that weren't magical, but for Willow, I would do anything.

I saw my own mistake now, far too late to change what had happened. I went up to our room and sat on the bed gently so as to not wake her, watching her sleep. Dark lashes rested against her creamy skin, and I could see a hint of a dark circle beneath her eyelids. She was tired. Her face was stained with tears and my heart twinged. I'd hurt her. My stupidity had hurt her, and it might have just cost us dearly.

The goods in the bag I'd left downstairs would provide us with anything we could ever possibly want, but we were about to be denied a multitude of worlds and experiences. My fingers itched to stroke her hair and I couldn't resist. I brushed a finger through her silky hair and felt love stir in my chest.

I'd spend the rest of my life making up for this mistake. I wouldn't let anything else stand in the way. Never again would I doubt her, or her decisions. She was a smart woman and had seen what the rest of us couldn't. Father had to be stopped before he destroyed us all. There was nothing he could do to take away her powers, he was a dragon and she was a hunter, after all, but he could make her forget that world. That didn't mean she'd forget the people there, or that my father had turned into a tyrannical madman.

We had a king. As such, he could be whatever he wanted to be, but we also had the ability to overthrow him if need be. Malcolm would make a much better king, and Arista an excellent queen. I would help however I could, to make sure that my home would be safe and continue to prosper. Whether we were meant to survive as a world remained to be seen, but our history showed that we must have a purpose. We'd survived millennia, we'd populated other realms on this planet, or the parallel universes as Willow called them. Worlds just beside each other, different in a variety of ways.

Each world had its own rules, its own magic, but my world was special to me because it was mine. Perhaps it had outlived its time. We didn't even have electricity in our world. Some might say we could live without radios, phones, and instant communications across the globe, but how much easier would it make life if we did have those things?

I sighed and stretched out beside my wife. We'd only been married for a couple of days now, and our lives had been turned upside down again. It wasn't fair to either of us, and I'd make this next transition as easy on Willow as I could. I left the bed as quietly as I came and started one of her favorite meals, spaghetti with her family's version of veggie-laden sauce. It was chunky style that I liked.

She came down about the time the garlic bread was ready to come out of the oven and just stared at me.

"You came back." I saw her gulp and her eyes were round.

"Did you think I wouldn't, princess?" I saw her eyes

brighten at the endearment. She had thought I wouldn't come! "Oh, my little love, I wouldn't leave you. Come, eat with me and then we'll talk about what's happened."

I led her to the table in the kitchen because we both found the dining room far too formal for our shared meals. I put a salad down on the table, her favorite salad dressing, and the rest of her food on a plate.

"You're spoiling me," she teased, her eyes happy and rarely leaving my face.

"I'll have to as that baby grows. Pregnant women need to be loved and cared for. I think, for a while, we'd almost forgotten about that baby. It's on the way though."

"At least I've missed morning sickness so far." She took a hefty bite of garlic bread and wrapped her spaghetti around her fork with a spoon as a base. I never understood why she did and used the edge of the fork to cut the noodles up into more manageable and far less messy pieces.

"That's something dragons usually don't have. Shifters either. It seems to be a human affliction."

"All I can say is, I'm glad I missed it. I've heard some horror stories and I have to admit, it was one of the reasons I didn't want to have a baby." She took another bite of her food as if she hadn't said something surprising.

"You didn't want children?" I couldn't fathom that, even the men in our world wanted children.

"Not really. My world is overpopulated and filled with unwanted children already. I didn't plan to marry or have children. It wasn't on my list of things to do."

"What did you want to do?"

"I wanted to compose, I wanted to play music, I wanted to experience life. I didn't want to have the same experience as my mother and aunts. Their men left them, right or wrong, and left them to raise their children on their own. It wasn't an easy life for any of us. I didn't want to do that to a child."

"I can see your reasons. Are you afraid I'll leave you on your own with our child?"

"I'm not afraid you'd choose to leave, no. Life isn't easy for women in my family." She looked like she wanted to say more but stopped.

"Mal's still with Arista and Galen." I pointed out.

"Yes, but will he always be? What if something happens? What if he dies?" Tears stung her eyes.

"Then the chain will continue. Would you rather not know the love we have, or what it's like to have Marya inside of you, with her precocious ways?"

"Oh, you should have heard her philosophizing to me earlier!" She looked so pleased and happy at the same time. "You took the right path, Willow, she said to me. Then she explained her existence, and what would happen after she was born. It was all sweet and enlightening really."

"That's just... breathtaking." I watched her as she talked about the baby and their conversation, seeing how happy it all made her. Yeah, I'd made the right decision, in the end.

"It is, really. She's so..." she squeezed her fists together for a minute, as if looking for a word but couldn't think of it.

"Enlightening?"

"Yes! That's the word."

"Do you still think life would be better without a child in it?" I asked, just to prolong the conversation. I was about to drop a bomb on her, but I wanted her to finish eating first.

"I think it's fine for some people. That's not my fate. My fate is to have this baby and be your wife," she answered soberly, but honestly.

"I can deal with that. So long as you don't regret anything that's happened?"

"I do regret influencing your father—"

I held a hand up. "No, we'll talk about that after dinner, princess. For now, eat."

We finished our meal then and cleaned up the kitchen. I took her by the hand and lit a fire outside, my dragon ability to light fire with a fingertip was still there, at least.

I waited, throughout dinner, throughout the cleanup, for the earth to tilt or to fall to the floor in pain, but nothing happened. That didn't mean it wouldn't, so I pulled Willow down to a lounger with me.

"I have to tell you a few things, darling. None of them will be easy to listen to, but you're my mate, and deserve nothing but the truth." I brushed her hair beneath my chin and rested my head on top of her head as I cradled her body. "Our world is about to change again."

19

WILLOW

$\mathcal{I}$ felt my body go still at his words and waited for him to go on. What now? What punishment had fate decided to mete out to us for being mates now? I wanted to scream, I wanted to kick and punch and hit something, but I had no idea what. Admittedly, our current mess was my fault.

"My father has banished you from my world. Your memories of my world will be erased, and you won't know how to return there. You may not even know about the dragons anymore." He took a deep breath before he carried on, without a minute to let me question him. "As a punishment to me for refusing to stand by him and to come to you instead, he's also sworn that I'll be stripped of my dragon and will become a mortal man."

"What the fuck, Henry?" I sat up and turned around

to look at my husband. "A mortal man? But, how can he do that to you? You are what it means to be a dragon."

"I don't know if he actually can. He tried quite a few things with Malcolm that failed. I think a lot of the time it's bluster and bluff to guilt us into doing what he wants. That or he has an exceptionally shitty magician."

"You don't look upset at all. I would think you'd be devastated by this." I reached out a hand to cup his cheek, but he just placed his hand over mine and smiled a beautiful, happy smile.

"I don't need to be a dragon, or magical, when I have you, Willow. My father gambled and lost when he made his threats. I could never turn you down, you're my mate. More importantly, I love you. I love you more than I love being a dragon, more than I love my own world. I'll just not be a party to raising our daughter to think she's not as good as a boy."

"Fuck that, she's going to be a badass, no matter what!"

"You've got that right." He pulled me to him for a kiss. It was full of joy and passion, two things that Godwin could not kill for us.

I had changed before I came down earlier and now had on a long white skirt and a light sweater my mom had knitted for me. Both were easy to remove, pull up, or push aside, and Henry eagerly pulled at the hem of the skirt to bare my thighs to his fingers.

He surprised me though, when he stood up and carried me into the house. We made it as far as the kitchen table before he dropped to his knees in front of me and pushed my skirt up around my hips.

I didn't think about the problems we had now, or what our future might hold if Henry stopped being a dragon, I just felt, and Henry worked to make sure I didn't have time to think about a thing. With strong fingers, he softly pushed my panties aside and spread my thighs so he could kneel between them.

I leaned back on the pine table and smiled at him. I put my hands under my head to act as a pillow as I felt his tongue delve into my folds with a greedy swipe. He delved deep between them to lick up the nectar that was always present when Henry was around.

"This is all we need, Willow. Each other." He swiped at me again and somehow it felt more, like it was far more pleasurable to have my husband's tongue in my pussy than it had ever been before. Probably a side effect of being pregnant, I decided, then stopped worrying about it because it felt too good to actually worry about.

I braced my feet on the table and used it as leverage to swivel my hips as he sucked my clit with a tight grip. I felt each suction as a jolt that traveled up my body and straight into my brain. Desire built inside me, a swelling, liquid thing that felt good but didn't feel like enough. It never felt like enough. When he slid two fingers into me, I started to pant, it was so close.

I rocked against his mouth and guided the way I wanted his tongue to flick at me with my movements. Henry alternated the way he tortured me, he'd suck at my clit until my fingers started to scratch at the table, and then he'd go back to long swipes. Henry was not in a rush, and I didn't want to be, but the upheaval had made me desperate for the oblivion only he could give me.

Henry didn't just use his tongue on me, though, his fingers slid into me in a rhythm that had me almost in tears with pleasure. My husband fucked me with his mouth, and with his fingers like he needed me to come more than I did. There was a desperate edge to his touch, as if he was afraid I'd disappear at any minute.

I reached down for him, but I couldn't reach anything but a hand he held up to me. I took it and gasped his name when he found the perfect rhythm between his teasing mouth and his maddening fingers. I'd never been inhibited around Henry, and I wasn't about to be now.

"Make me come, Henry. Fuck, baby, please, I need it. Make me come." My words ended harshly as he fucked his fingers into me harder, deeper, and sucked my clit just a little more tightly.

Henry groaned against my clit as I begged him for

relief and the vibration finally sent me over the edge. He didn't stop when I gasped suddenly, or when I stopped breathing because there was only pleasure and I didn't need air anymore. He didn't stop when I finally gasped in a long breath on a groan of pleasure so deep I felt like I shattered into a million pieces.

Henry didn't stop until I pushed at his head. He let me have every moment of selfish pleasure I wanted to take, and I took quite a few moments to revel in that solitary plain where only *good* existed. He didn't say a word, just stared into my eyes as he unbuttoned his pants. He pushed the uniform, his father's uniform, away and I knew he'd never put it on again.

He let his gaze travel down my body, his fingers lingering on the bulge of my stomach, and he smiled before he tore my panties away. He lifted my ass after I was bare, just enough to position me just right.

There, on our kitchen table, my husband plunged into me in one smooth, sharp thrust. We both gasped as he sank to the hilt inside of me. We knew what was coming, it never changed, but the path to that final moment of oneness could vary. I felt every second of his entry, the way he opened me and filled me made me shiver.

It wasn't always about the bump and grind, sometimes, it was about the acts before, during, and after. Henry understood that, and he gave me a moment to savor how it felt to be filled by him before he pushed into me again. He pulled out, and even that was a new act of pleasure as I felt every line and ridge of him scrape against my inner walls in a pleasurable way. I tore the panels of his shirt open—he'd never wear that again either—and pushed the now offensive garment away. My hands ran down strong shoulders, over the rigid muscles in his chest and down his hard abdomen, every inch just another muscle, until I found the spot where we were joined.

I grasped two fingers around him and gave a moan of delight as I felt the way he pistoned into me with my now slick fingers. I'd never done that before, I don't know what drove me to do it now, but it delighted both of us, so I didn't stop. I still had my clothes on, but I didn't care as I leaned up to look at what exactly Henry was doing to my body.

I couldn't really see, so I spread my legs a little wider, and there, before my eyes, I could see the way that Henry slid into me smoothly, and the way his cock gleamed with my juices. I moaned and parted my lips. I wanted to clean every speck of me off him but knew that right now, a bomb going off would not stop Henry as he fucked us both into another plane.

"This is all we need, Willow. We need to fuck each other until we can't walk. We need to talk to each other until our problems are solved. Most of all, all we need is my dick in this fucking tight pussy of yours to make us forget the world exists. Because it doesn't if we don't let it." He spoke to me through a clenched jaw, his eyes wide as he continued to fuck into me harder, faster.

I settled back and joined him in that place where his soul brushed against mine. It was a tease in its own way, the way our souls danced around each other until one or the other sucked into the white of one or the blue of the other. No matter who took in the other first, the end result would be the same, a light blue smoky soul, the oneness that was us.

His hips worked into me, and his fingers dug into my ass tighter to tilt me at a different angle, the one he knew would be the end of me, the end of my struggle to explode. "Henry!"

"That's right, princess, come with me, baby. Come for me."

My body pulsed, his pulsed, and together we swirled into oneness again.

The world fell away, and I was Henry, and Henry was me. I felt the relief flood me as his juices shot from his body and into mine, as if I really was him. He felt the way my inner walls fluttered, the way my stomach rippled, and the uncontrollable way my back arched as something shot up my spine, through my chest, and straight into my brain. This wasn't just a cute little flutter of some naughty muscles, and then a sigh of relief.

Oh no, it never was with Henry. He worked at me, he made me come, there was no, yeah that was nice baby, with him. Nope, you either had your mind blown or you didn't stop. And he wouldn't. He'd let me have a few on my own sometimes because he knew we both enjoyed the solitary orgasm every now and then, but most of the time, he knew we both needed this.

We swirled together, pleasured beyond just sex. Every cell of my being felt good, every cell of his being was mine, and those felt good as well. Not good, oh that's nice, no this was *good.* Like chocolate-lava cake with whipped cream and more chocolate-fudge-sauce-on-your-tongue-exploding-your-taste-buds-on-crack good.

We had to come down eventually, and it was clear that neither of us wanted to leave that place. Who would? Chocolate lava cake on crack good, remember? Only an idiot would want to leave that.

We came back to the world together, both of us exhausted but happy. He helped me up and took me to the living room to sit on the couch while he prepared two glasses of apple juice.

"What do you want to do tomorrow, princess?" He settled beside me and I looked at him with wide eyes.

"I don't think I'm a princess anymore, am I?" It didn't really upset me if I wasn't.

"Of course you are. We'll live longer than Godwin, I expect, and Malcolm will undo anything Father's done that he doesn't agree with." He looked uncertain for a moment. "If he disagrees with him on it."

"He might agree that I overstepped a line."

"He might. But Arista will talk him around. She's always been able to talk sense into that man, even when the rest of us couldn't."

"Do you think a war is coming?" It was time for serious talk, and I asked the one question that weighed on my mind.

"I don't know. Something is happening in my world, in your world too. Maybe I should contact the Alexander brothers, find out what's happening there."

"If you're stuck here you might as well. You're a soldier, babe, it's what you do. You might as well do it for them."

"I think I will. As long as you're alright with that?"

"I am, I'd like to get to know those ladies of theirs a little better. I think they all have a rather intriguing story to tell."

"I imagine they do. I'm not traveling anywhere until Marya makes her appearance, though, so if they want to use me, they'll have to come to me."

He pulled me close, wrapped a blanket around us

both, and we watched the moon rise in the sky together. The world was an uncertain place, but one thing was solid as a rock for both of us. No matter what, the only thing that mattered was each other.

It was hard to believe I'd hated him so much in the beginning. I couldn't imagine life without him now. That bragging asshole had disappeared, and the real man had shone through. I loved who he was: a strong man, both in mind and body, he was intelligent, capable, and all mine.

"I love you, Henry. If you'd told me when I first met you that one day I'd have your baby in my belly, and your name on my lips with every word I spoke, I'd have laughed at you. We've both changed so much."

He kissed the top of my head, and I heard him chuckle. "You left out the part where, if I'd said it, I'd have been right."

I pinched him in the ribs and we laughed, and that laugh turned into a kiss. The kiss turned into a burn of passion that neither of us ever seemed to get enough of. I don't think we ever will.

20

EDANA

I walked up to the house, the house of my cousin, with a pang of regret in my heart. She was about to have the family I'd never have. My job wouldn't allow for the time it would take to find a husband, produce a child, and then get back to work. My job was so demanding I'd never see the baby anyway.

I glanced around the place, looking for threats, though I doubted there were any. It was a habit from my job, one I couldn't stop, even when I was off duty. I had to put that part of me behind me for now though. Willow was in that house giving birth and Aleric was going to be there. He and his siblings had been given leave to visit their brother and his wife by their dickhead of a father.

Godwin, the man that plagued us all, for one reason

or another. His time was coming though, I know that for a fact.

Aleric and I took every opportunity we could to see each other. I couldn't resist the younger man, no matter how much I might try. There'd been no sex, or even real touches, but I knew it was in the cards. There was no turning down the mating call when it found you and he was my mate, I didn't need him or anybody else to tell me that. I knew it like I knew my own name.

We'd have dinner together, or watch a movie, maybe go out for a drink, but we'd never had a moment alone, I made sure of that. Once we mated, the draw to always be together would be much stronger. I might want him, I might need him like I needed breath, but I had a job to do, and right now, that didn't include being mated. First, I wanted to see this baby and find out what Willow had brought into the world.

I walked into the house when Rachel let me in and went up the stairs to where I could hear loud voices. Aleric was already there, I felt his eyes on me when I walked in but didn't acknowledge he was there. Everything was done now, and the baby was in a bassinet by her mother's bed.

"Marya is it?" I asked as a greeting to them all.

"That's her name, yes. I'm glad you came, Edana. I've missed you." Willow looked exhausted but happy. I suppose that's how I'd look if I let Aleric take this as far as he wanted to.

He didn't push for it though. He was a gentleman in every way, that man. I leaned over to look at the baby, pink and perfect and wonderful. Her little newborn blue eyes were gleaming up at me as I looked down at her, but I saw the flash of the dragon there. Interesting.

I was about to look away, to ask Willow how she was, but I saw something that stopped me. From the baby's finger, a light pink spark had burned for just a second before it dimmed out. Had I imagined it? I watched but it didn't happen again. Maybe it had all been a trick of the light.

"She's amazing, Willow." I didn't know what else to say, I've never been to see a newborn or even to a baby shower.

Once I'd left my home at 18 I'd thrown myself into my training, and then into my job. There were no friends to go and visit, I didn't live near any family, and after a while, I blocked the ones that remained from my mind. I had a very important job, and it didn't involve cooing over babies and making new mothers feel proud. That had all changed when the dragons showed up and my family gave me the perfect cover to find out more about them.

I'd reconnected with the family when Willow wanted me to come to her wedding. Now, I had far more than

I'd bargained for. I couldn't tell any of them about my real job, or about what I did, or why I was even really there.

It wasn't all the baby, or even about Aleric. It was to gather information about the dragons.

I made certain the mental steel trap I had around my brain was in place and watched those around me. All of my family that was left, and most of Henry's family was there. Four magnificent dragons, all in one place. Five if you counted baby Galen. Six if Marya was indeed a dragon too.

Not a single full dragon in my entire career had been found, but now, now there were at least five of them within my sights. I'd have never dreamed it possible.

"Edana, care for a drink?" Aleric called out to me and I quickly agreed.

I followed him down the stairs and to the kitchen. I watched him as he moved. He was tall, well-muscled, and handsome. The Greek god Adonis in the flesh, if such a god had ever existed. If he had, he'd have looked just like the younger man in front of me.

He was a serious man, Aleric, but he could laugh too. So far, I'd learned he was intelligent, poetic, and passionate about life in general. His gaze on my body could set me on fire, an accidental touch could turn that fire into an uncontrolled blaze. I was made of stronger stuff than my cousin though, and with my training? Well, I'd be able to hold out for a while.

"I'd like you to come away with me this weekend," he said as he poured two glasses of wine from the fridge. He knew I liked white and had chosen that from the bottles available.

"You know I can't just disappear, Aleric. I have to be in contact." I started but he didn't let me finish.

"I know, I know, your work." He sighed and pushed out of the back door. The air was cold at this time of year, and I snatched a shawl Willow had left on a hook at the door.

"It's not that I wouldn't like to spend more time with you, it's just that my job is important. I can't just abandon it."

"I understand. I would like to spend more time with you though. I'd like to see the moonlight on your face as you sleep and the sunlight on your hair when you wake up." He turned and his hand came up to touch my face, but I stepped back.

"Maybe one day, Aleric. I just..." I paused, how to put him off this time. "I don't want to rush things."

"Because you're older? Is that the problem?" He looked down at me, an easy task for most men, but for him, it was a long way down.

"No, yes. I don't know, I haven't really thought about that aspect much." I suppose it did bother me a little, but he was my mate, it would stop mattering the moment we had sex.

That was the real problem. I didn't want to lose myself in anyone. Mates eventually became so entangled in their oneness that the rest of the world played second fiddle. That could be dangerous when your job was to protect others.

"Then why won't you let me melt every bone in your body for you, Edana?" The way he said my name nearly made my knees melt, the fucker!

I looked at him with narrowed eyes. Had he done that on purpose, added that lilt to sound sexy?

All of the dragons had an accent, somewhere between Irish and English, and the way the vowels of my name rolled off his tongue was a drug on its own.

"I just need time, Aleric. I have to have things in place and to be ready for it."

"Arista and Willow didn't have that opportunity. Neither did Mal and Henry for that matter. Why should we?"

"Because we aren't them, Aleric. You're special to me, and I want what I know is coming, believe me I do." I pulled the shawl tighter around my shoulders. The cold had suddenly penetrated much deeper than I thought it would. "I just need time, okay?"

He didn't seem to like that idea, but there wasn't anything he could do about it. Or so I thought. I thought that was the end of the conversation and turned to walk back into the house to get out of the cold. A whoosh and the sudden sensation of the world falling away was the only warning I had before the world really did fall away.

Then, I was in the sky, black claws more massive than anything I'd ever seen on a living animal grasped around me to cradle me to a black leather wall. Aleric had shifted! He'd also pulled me into the air with him.

"Aleric!" I screamed his name, but the wind tore the word from my lips before they even really made a sound.

We were high in the clouds, so far up I was afraid I wouldn't be able to breathe, but something helped my lungs to remain functional. Maybe it was my own genes. I wasn't sure, but I clung to his black claws in terror. My head told me he wouldn't drop me, but my stomach said he might.

A knot of fear twisted there, and I closed my eyes to block it all out. I was afraid of heights on normal days. This was enough to make my brain go into overdrive. After another moment, it did, and the world went dark.

When the world came back into focus we were in a small cabin somewhere cold, really cold. A lantern chased shadows on the walls, and I saw no electric lights anywhere. In fact, there was no telephone, computer, or even an electric can opener in sight.

A fire burned in a fireplace across the room from me,

and I sat up to find I was on a queen-sized bed. A threadbare quilt covered the mattress, and the furniture in the room looked as if it came out of a 1970s sitcom with garish taste. But then, wasn't everything from the 70s garish?

"Aleric?" I called out, but there was no answer. I got out of the bed and pushed open the only door that didn't look like it led outside. It opened into a small bathroom with a cast iron tub covered in white enamel, and a toilet that looked to be one of the first models introduced, and a utilitarian sink. What the hell was this place? A handyman's fantasyland of secondhand shop heaven?

"Aleric?" I called out when I didn't find him in there. I went to the door that led outside and looked out.

A frozen wasteland greeted me. Mountains and snow, that's all I saw. Not even trees. Just mountains and snow.

"Where the hell have you brought me, dragon?" I wandered around until I felt the cold through the leather of my work shoes and went back to the porch. If you could call it a porch. It was little more than a wide space, three-foot-wide by four-foot-long.

"Aleric!" I called out his name loudly and I saw him come from the back of the cabin with a smile on his face. "You utter bastard! What have you done?!"

I launched myself at him. My hands came up to give

him a punch that would knock him on his ass, but he deflected it easily, and dropped the load of wood in his arms to pull me tight to his body. I wasn't sure if it was to stop my blows or to kiss me, maybe it had started out as a defense tactic, but before long, my struggles turned into fists curled into his coat to hold him against me, and I reached up on tiptoes to fuse my lips to his.

The world narrowed down to that point and even the bitter cold that bit into any skin that wasn't covered disappeared. There was only Aleric and the sweet pull of his lips against mine.

"Edana..." He breathed my name against my cheek, when he slid his lips from mine. "Go in the house, it's too cold out here."

"I'm only obeying because you're right, it's fucking cold out here. Come inside." He stomped in behind me to disburse the snow from his boots after he picked up the wood he'd dropped.

He set a few pieces on the fire before he turned back to me.

"I'm sorry. Please don't be mad, but I was out of ideas. This seemed, romantic. Fitting." His eyes, an enchanting baby blue, held my gaze and I forgot the dirty names I wanted to call him. That kiss!

Damn him, that kiss might very well have broken me. At last.

"Where are we?" I demanded, adding an acid note of anger to my voice.

"Russia. Or Tibet. It might even be Canada. Or Norway. I have no idea, really. I'm not sure. I just kind of chose a place. This place was empty, and I couldn't smell humans on it anymore, so I thought it would work. There's a huge wood supply in the back, a cross that I think is your sign for graves in this world, and nothing else. I'll have to fly down for more food at some point, but for now, what I found while you slept will work."

"While I slept? How long was I asleep?" I looked outside. I'd thought the falling darkness was a sign of the time zone that we were in, but now I wasn't sure.

"About 12 hours. I stayed with you for the first eight, but when you kept sleeping I went out for things we might need. Food, beverages, more blankets, toiletries. Things like that."

"So let me get this right. You kidnapped me, first of all." I glared at him, but he didn't even pretend to be ashamed of himself. Instead, he gave me a very naughty grin. I squinted my eyes a little more. "Then you bring me to a cabin and you have no idea where we are. Then, then you tell me that we have supplies. Does that mean we're going to be here for a while, young man?"

I broke out the old lady routine on him, but it only made that naughty grin tilt in an even saucier way.

"We can leave whenever you like, Edana. As long as you agree to spend more time with me."

"I can't believe this! Take me home!" I stood up from the bed again and glared down at him by his place near the fire.

"We're mates, Edana. You are my mate, my dragon halfling. Why do you insist on fighting it?"

I stepped back as he revealed my own secret to the world by giving it a name. How much did he really know about me? If my blood wasn't still hot from that kiss I might be worried. But that sensual grin only spread a little bit wider, and that made my blood heat up all over again. I was in so much trouble. So much fucking trouble!

ABOUT THE AUTHOR

Selina Coffey is a romance writer who lives happily in London with her husband and son. She is a hopeless romantic who grew up always believing in love and she is not ashamed to admit this! It is this belief that makes her so passionate about writing crazy love stories.

A stereotypical girly girl, she loves shopping. So whenever she gets a chance and the spare cash, you will probably find her browsing online for the next pair of shoes to add to her collection.!

You can find her online at
www.selinacoffey.com

Contact her at
hello@selinacoffey.com

www.ingramcontent.com/pod-product-compliance
Lightning Source LLC
Chambersburg PA
CBHW031235210726
48287CB00003B/787